MW01047155

TORRENTS OF OUR TIME
Twenty-Two Stories

Christian Fennell

F i r e n z e   B o o k s
NYC • Washington, D.C. • Toronto

The Real and the Imagined
Trilogy

ISBN: 9781777281007

Torrents of Our Time/Christian Fennell—1st edition.
The Real and the Imagined, Book One

Any references to historical events, real people, or real places are used fictitiously. Names, characters, and places are products of the author's imagination.

Front cover art: Carolina Himmel
www.boutiquedeartedecarolinah.mitiendanube.com

F i r e n z e   B o o k s
NYC • Washington, D.C. • Toronto
firenzebooks.com

www.christianfennell.com

Jan, Mackenzie, Cael, Ty, Rachael

"I am certain of nothing but of the holiness of the heart's affections and the truth of the imagination."

—John Keats

TABLE OF CONTENTS

"The word is a flame burning in a dark glass."
— Sheila Watson

UNDER A BIG MOON

She came out there, and the young girl, Rachael, looked at the state-sponsored woman. I saw her from my window. It was dark but there was a big moon and she was wearing her long white nightgown.

She went into the garage?

Yes, and Rachael pushed off the ground with her foot, pulling back on the chains, the swing going, the rusted chains squeaking.

The too-dark garage, afraid to turn the light on, afraid to wake them, and so she stumbled, even though she knew where it was— exactly where it was, that which she had come for, and would not put off. Not anymore.

Was she there a long time?

Rachael looked at the garage, the squeak of the chains slowing.

Rachael?

She looked at the woman. She looked back at the garage. She had something in her hand, but I couldn't see what it was.

In the dark she reached the workbench and placed a pitcher of lemonade and ice on it. She bent down and looked beneath the bench, her hand searching for, and then finding, that which she had come for. She struggled to lift it with one hand and bent over more, using both hands to place it on the bench.

1

The swing was hardly moving now, just drifting, slowly, back and forth, as if there was a big moon up there, that very same moon, and it was dark, and it was quiet, and she was alone and waiting, and she'd say, Momma. She looked at the woman. At her long hair. Her nice clothes.

Your momma?

Yes.

She looked past the woman at the house. I think Daddie's upset because he was supposed to be watching her.

Is that what he said?

No, but I know he was.

Why?

Because he left his job so he could.

He was a teacher?

Yes, the only one and he taught us all.

Who's the teacher now?

It's a lady, but I don't go, so I don't know. My daddie teaches me here.

He does?

Yes, mostly, but not every day.

Was your daddie sleeping when your momma went outside?

He didn't wake up until we heard her fall in the hallway.

She left the garage?

Yes.

Sitting on the high wooden stool, her legs crossed, she sipped a mixed drink of lemonade and antifreeze. And in the dim blue light of the moon slipping through the side door window, she stared into the darkness of new hope, and she began to hum, "You are my sunshine, my only sunshine. You make me happy, when skies are grey. You'll never know, dear, how much I love you." And she hummed on, her foot tapping on, the music in her head—playing on, and she forced down another sip.

I should get supper goin.

I can give you a hand.

That's all right.

No, I'd like too, if that's all right?

Did your daddie talk to you about your momma?

Not too much. Would you like a cup of tea?

Yes, please.

I'll put the kettle on.

Thank you.

You're welcome. He just said, did I know she died of a broken heart?

A broken heart?

Yes, that's what he said. Because the world made her sad.

I'm sorry.

That's okay. But it wasn't just the world that made her sad.

It wasn't?

No. She told me why.

She did?

Yes. She said, sometimes she got sad because another world, not this one, another one, would come and settle upon her. But I wasn't to worry because it would never come for me. She said she just knew, and I would be okay. She promised.

She said that?

Yes.

She promised?

Yes.

Do you worry about that?

She looked at the woman. The pretty, state sponsored woman. With her nice hair. Her nice clothes.

Rachael?

She heard her name, but she wasn't there, she was on her swing.

3

Under a big moon.
That very same moon.
In the dark, in the quiet, waiting.
That calling. That pulling. The chains squeaking.

INTRODUCTION:
WHY I WRITE FICTION

How do we use this space—this time, you and I, best? What do we have to say? Because that's what it is, isn't it? Like a train on a track in a needle—running. Time. Understanding. This place and love. We all have this and we all want this.

For the longest time I couldn't write directly about mental health. I still can't, not really, not comfortably, and most certainly, not particularly well. Not as someone who suffers from it, but as someone who lived and loved next to it.

And so I found fiction. Or more accurately, fiction found me. And that was enough, more than enough, because I didn't really want it there all the time, either. It was like that train on a track—there it is again, running.

Realism as writing, a retelling, is far too often a false witness. It's filtered and constrained, our need for context and perspective far too great. Wanting. Needing. It's not me. It's you. And yet, with the passing of time, with hindsight and contextual perspective, the details drift.

"Memory is a poet, not a historian." Marie Howe.

Fiction is truth. Or rather, as Albert Camus said, "Fiction is the lie through which we tell the truth." Remembered realism? Little more than a dream. For how can we trust the mirror from which we retell our stories?

Both can be powerful.

Both can be painful.

But what is honest?

With nonfiction, we are trapped within our points of view, our objectivity never always being just that. Our retelling, always never more than what we know, or think we know—a weakness in the heart of everyone's truth.

With fiction, we sidestep these pitfalls of the rational mind, allowing for the insights of our intuitive thinking, our hands guided by the enlightenment of our trust. Freed from the captivity of the mighty "I," we are capable of reaching far beyond that which can only be discovered through our constrained selves, a place where truth can come, unconstrained; it just might not be the truth we thought we knew, or wanted to know.

I am a witness, and I am a participant, and yet, life is so much more than that too. It has to be. And it's this separation I find difficult, the blurred lines of our lives and the unraveling of them.

How do we objectively separate ourselves from this?

From love?

From pain?

How do we write best about that which can't be known?

Fiction allows for this, it craves it, on its way to greater truths. Nonfiction rejects it.

"The need of reason is not inspired by the quest for truth but by the quest for meaning. And truth and meaning are not the same thing. The basic fallacy, taking precedence over all specific metaphysical fallacies, is to interpret meaning on the model of truth." Hannah Arendt.

And so I write fiction, to try to escape the condensed thinking of the modern mind, the endless need for defining, for meaning, this understanding of "self." Because I don't need that—I reject it, surrendering to the idea it's just not knowable, in any trustworthy manner.

With fiction, I am able to try to seek, by removing myself as much as possible, an unbiased, unintentional truth, no matter what that truth might be.

"I think life would be pretty boring if we understood everything. It's better if we don't understand anything . . . and know that we don't, that's the important part." Noam Chomsky.

YOU ARE A CHILD
OF GOD TOO

Lizzy is down by the stream by the big trees by the muddy bank, the leaves moving away, and there comes a small breeze now.

Buster Parker?

In the tall grass.

In the shade.

Lizzy. His hand is on a damp stump and there are bugs and it smells punky. He moves away, closer to Lizzy on the other side of the stream.

Can you feel that—oh, and there's mushrooms. Zander, look at the mushrooms.

There is blood on her white nightgown.

Lizzy.

I hav'ta find my bear.

It's by the big rock, I saw ya do it.

All the little feet sinking in the ever-mossy ground.

Buster Parker?

And now a voice comes with the breeze up from the downstream: And you, Lizzy, you are a child of God too.

In the silence by the woods by the stream she is there. Why Zander? Why do we hav'ta go now?

I told ya already, ya know why. C'mon now.

His bare feet find the dirty sticky floor, his elbows his knees, his hands rubbing his face and moving through his hair. He exhales to the late morning boozy air and leans back, his thin white chest and arms poxed with the markings of a man burning in the certainty of this place, of this heat. He reaches for his cigarettes and lights one. He puts the lighter back on the nightstand and leans forward and closes his eyes and takes a drag. His body is rank with destruction, and he knows it. But it won't always be, not always. He opens his eyes and exhales, drifting blue smoke heavy in the hot dead air. He looks up. Fuck, he says.

They walk in the woods, little and lost, the Spanish moss their covering. By the stream. Always stay to the stream.

Where are we goin?

I told ya already. I've told ya a hundred times.

Tell me again then.

California.

Oh, California. Is that far?

Yes it is, it's far.

But I'm tired now.

They cross a dirt road and there's a thin man wearing a straw trilby hat riding a bike backward. He's old, with beautiful olive skin. Squinty eyes. He looks and smiles and Lizzy does too.

They walk on and soon they come to an open field. A young boy is there. He has long blond hair, long past his shoulders. He's short, maybe Lizzy's age, and there's a dog.

Looks like a wolf. What's your name?

Ty.

My name's Lizzy. Where are ya goin, Ty?

Nowhere.

What'ya mean nowhere?

The little boy points south in the wide open field of that day, the beautiful tall grass, the sun hard upon it, a strong scent of alfalfa.

Lizzy looks to where he points and there's a small girl sitting in the moving grass, her back to them, her long full hair falling away.

Lizzy.

I have to say goodbye to Ty.

Who's Ty?

Never mind. Goodbye, Ty.

But he is gone—and there he is, walking more yet down from the northlands, the dog out front, easy breezy, Lizzy thinks. Bye-bye little girl.

They continue walking, beneath a low heavy sky, the Spanish moss shaded, and it is weeping.

Can you hear that?

Shh.

These bushes are prickly.

Quiet, Lizzy. Look, it's a monkey.

Sitting on a stump he lowers his harp. He turns and looks. A broad smile. A gold tooth. He leans forward. If I'm a monkey, he says, then I'm the Monkey King, and he laughs, a bigger than all the world laugh, in the wind, his harp music again, long and lonely and forever still, over the sounds of the streamy water.

He walks into the kitchen—there had better be some fuckin coffee. He picks up a small pot from the cluttered mess on the counter and looks inside. He puts it down and picks up another one and looks inside of it.

She comes, wrapping her arms around him, from the back of him, her sticky crisp blond hair in her face pressing to his back. Where are the kids at?

How the hell should I know? Outside. Make some damn coffee.

11

She sucks her breath in, this fear brought to her, such a man as this, a Monkey King man, and he stands, taller than us all.

Come along now, and he turns and walks in the woods, his bare feet, his white cotton shirt opened at the neck, big baggy pants with a wide leather belt. He stops and looks back. You mustn't be staying out here. Not here.

You can do it, Lizzy, go on, you can walk in these woods, like that, with this man. Come along, Zander, we can do it, we can walk in these woods, with this man, take my hand and don't let go. And don't you worry, Lizzy, don't you worry one bit, we'll find your bear and keep it safe. We promise we will.

They walk upon a path known only to the man before them. And why were they? Walking in these woods alone with a man like that and not a single friend there to walk with them even though it was daylight and these woods were the same woods. And where were they going—oh, California, and maybe this way was the right way and all the days of blue skies were just about upon them.

Zander puts his hand to Lizzy's shoulder, his recent markings on his arm, the blood there dried and dark, bright red around the etching: 18 88 14. Let's go back.

No, we mustn't.

The man stops and looks around, for what they wonder? They look too. For all the little lost children of the woods. And these woods were silent. He looks at Lizzy and Zander, his words coming to them as if not in need of the very air carrying them. We're almost there now, it's not far.

He sits on the porch step, his coffee mug in his hand, his white and pink skin, his markings, his fear, not unlike all the others, there and for all the world to see, and he thinks—but no, he cannot. Not that.

Lizzy.

His camp is at the crux of where a shallow stream cuts away from the Tidewater River, a wide hard-packed shoreline of smooth stones and sand. At the edge of the trees there's a shelter made of branches open to the southeast, filled with leaves and pine needles and covered in the skin of a black bear.

The hare is cut into strips of meat cooking upright on green willow branches surrounding the open fire.

The Monkey King reaches to the edge of the coals and picks out a mud-packed ear of corn and Zander winces at the imagined pain of the hot coals.

They watch him blow baked mud embedded with orange embers away from the burnt husk of corn.

They eat their meal, not speaking, the sun falling.

The Monkey King slides a piece of rabbit from the stick. Like the Mighty Z, he says, born of this world, and yet, is the world itself.

What's the Mighty Z? asks Lizzy.

It's just a theory.

What theory? asks Zander.

The more you get to the end of everything—the end of your faith, your beliefs, your knowing—that is what is there, and waiting. Back to the very end again.

Lizzy smiles. The Mighty Z.

That's right, Lizzy. Do you suppose this hare liked being a hare?

Yes, says Lizzy. He was a nice hare.

Yes, he was, but it knowing it was a hare, or not a hare, did not change it from being this hare. He looks at the children, and they are silent, and he leans back and laughs, his bigger than all the world laugh. We need music, and he plays on. The fire burning on, his wide eyes holding them as he plays, looking, and looking again, and beyond them, this man, the Monkey King man, playing for all the little lost children of the woods. The fire burning on, twists of grey smoke and orange embers pushing up his notes, a warm southern breeze taking them away.

She steps from the porch, a light summer dress on, barefoot, and she walks across the short dead grass, stepping around discarded items of some past wanting. She stops at the end of the yard and looks at the shaded woods and the stream where she does not like to go.

Lizzy. Zander.

She crosses her arms as if she were cold in that dead flat heat.

Lizzy.

Her hands digging into her arms, squeezing.

Zander.

Not even a breeze to welcome her words.

Lizzy. Zander.

Just their names.

Standing at the stove cooking off cocaine, he turns and looks out the screen door, and in the coming dark he can hear his wife again: Lizzy. Zander.

He put the children to bed and covers them in the heaviness of the bearskin, and he sits and watches, Zander, sleeping, but not Lizzy, her eyes wide still, outwaiting the pain in the night, in the coming dark, and he puts his hand to her forehead—there there now—now now, and she squeezes her fists and she closes her eyes and she flees again, a little girl on the back of duskywings.

The sheriff's here.

Go on out and talk to him, I'll be out in a minute.

She steps onto the porch, the screen door slapping shut behind her, the evening heat coming to her.

The car stops.

She watches him get out of the car.

Kerry.

Sheriff.

He walks around the car and leans against the front of it. Where's Edward at?

She looks back over her shoulder.

We checked at the school, nobody's seen em.

No?

Alice said they never got on the bus.

Buttoning his shirt up, Edward walks out the door. Sheriff.

She looks at her husband. They never got on the bus.

We checked with Alice, the sheriff tells Edward.

They'll be hearing about this, that's for damn sure.

Any problems lately? Last night, say?

Nope, none. He looks at his wife.

She looks at her husband. She looks back at the sheriff. Nothin like that, no.

The sheriff looks back at the woods. You check in there?

Yup, nothin, says Edward.

She looks to the woods and crosses her arms.

The sheriff pushes off the car. We'll talk to folks in town case they show up there. In the meantime, if you think of anything, or they show back here, let us know.

She watches the sheriff get in the car, back it up, and pull away. She looks at her husband, leaning past the broken porch railing and spitting to the dry dirt.

He sits in the dark watching over them still. Lizzy sleeping. Her crying, dried and fallen, the rattling of her hollowing, fear chewing bones and soft tissue, all of it coming to him and settling heavy upon him. He leans forward and whispers, never again, my dear, Lizzy. Never again.

She opens her eyes.

He smiles.

Lizzy, looking off somewhere else.

It's me.

She looks at the Monkey King man.

We've known each other a long time, Lizzy. A real long time. We're friends.

Buster! And she folds herself into the enormous size of him, the good covering of him.

My little Lizzy.

You came for me.

Of course I did, I've never not been here. You know that. Time stretches all the way back to when we were the very same, and then before that, and again before that—it's a continuum. Of course it is, and you can remember that too, if ya wanted to.

Zander awake in the dark with them, and whoever knows what is out there, waiting? What'ya mean we were the same?

He looks at Zander.

Not the same color we weren't.

Yes, Zander.

What color?

That original man and me, the one and the very same.

That's a lie, and you know it. We weren't nev'r niggers.

Zander! And Lizzy looks at her brother.

The Monkey King, smiling, leans closer to Zander, his eyes widening, the whites of them upon him, and he puts his hand to Zander's face, Zander squinting at the touch, at the hum that comes. We're the same, Zander, despite what you think, or think it ought to be, or what you've been told.

How come we're not still then?

The Monkey King looks to the dark and what he sees there. Geography and a nomadic curiosity, I suppose. A need to survive. That and a happy, ever-loving, ongoing resilience. He looks back at the children. Our bodies are wonderful things and capable of such great change. Like the earth itself. He looks again to the darkness, at the river, at the moon reflecting upon the low rippling section. What'ya say we cool down?

In the night, from the porch, she calls again: Lizzy. Zander. And from the darkness, there is no answer.

They're on their backs, gripping and holding wet rocks under the moonlight, the clear cool water running over them.

Close your eyes and let go. Let it take you, and the Monkey King stretches his arms behind him, his hands to the water. Do not be afraid. And they do. Can you feel it? They smile and he smiles, his gold tooth reflecting the moonlight, and they're quiet, only the sounds of the water running over them, the good feel of it—the endless room within it. Everything we know, or think we know, is going, it's changing, like the very rocks beneath us. Our ability to do so is our freedom. And we must embrace it and never turn our backs to it. Never.

Lizzy closes her eyes and smiles. She's never gonna move away from this spot, right here. Never.

The children tucked in and sleeping, he walks in the woods, the moon and the quiet with him, the empty and the dark, and he reaches out to the undercurrent of restless stillness before him, the long reaching sounds of the South. He looks at the moon, his hands in his pockets now, and he walks on, without thought, unconcerned, and he begins to hum.

At the edge of town he stops.

He walks up the last gravel road before the asphalt streets. He comes to a laneway and walks up it.

He stops and looks at the house.

The woman is stretched out on the couch, these killing of endless maddening moments of time, unable to touch her now.

He stops at an open bedroom door. Edward is there, still in his pants, asleep on top of the blankets.

He bends over the man, tilting his head, and Edward wakes, his eyes widening at the sight of the Monkey King's large black face before him.

He wraps his massive hand around Edward's neck and squeezes. Edward kicks, he can't breathe, his hands coming to the Monkey King's hand.

He lifts the man and he puts him over his shoulder and walks out of the door.

The man's not dead, riding lifeless on the Monkey King's shoulder.

He walks across the yard and opens the small wooden gate and crosses the creek. He comes to a tall pine tree with a broken branch and he lifts the man by his shoulders, holding him out before him, and he says, in my weakness lives the world, and he presses the man to the sharp broken branch, the branch pushing out from the man's chest. He steps back and looks at the man hanging from the tree. Never again, my dear Lizzy. Never again.

He moves barefoot, quiet, dark in the dark, through the woods. And now the water, the cold creek water. He's moving in it, and there's a mist, the water coming harder and faster, and he stops and stands, the water breaking to him, rising, moving faster yet, the mist heavier, and like a hell-boy, the sky cracks, rolling in its opening, the desire of lightning welcoming back to itself the source, the wind heavy in its coming, cracking trees and breaking limbs, big birds flying, and he tilts his head back and opens his mouth and it comes furious, this fury, disastrous and beautiful in its origin, and there, and coming, and always coming harder, and he eats it all.

Upstream the thin man wearing the straw trilby hat watches.

And in the moving branches of the trees, in the quiet under the moonlight, we hear his voice once again: You are a child of God too.

For there is only love and there is mercy.

His harp music again, long and lonely and forever still, over the sounds of the streamy water.

AN OLD MAN AND A BOY:
SAMUEL'S STORY

The hole smells of buried roots and old dirt.

River water running.

A screaming.

The boy there, and he hears his mother yelling no.

She's crying.

The baby in his arms crying, struggling, and he holds her tighter.

The sounds of his mother stopping.

The struggling baby crying harder.

Shh, he whispers, they'll hear you, and he puts his hand to her mouth.

It's quiet, and he waits and he listens, pressing himself back farther into the dark earthy hole, holding the baby in his arms tighter, squeezing harder, his hand upon her mouth.

He's an old man, short and thin with uneven clumps of white hair, his face smudged with dirt and heavily lined and red, as if constantly exposed to a cold wind. He stands in the river, unmoving, his deep-set, squinting eyes, focusing on a small collection of flies and spiders he's placed on the still water. He hears a sound and looks. He places the pole he's holding on the grassy, muddy shoreline, and he unsheathes his knife.

He crosses the river at the low rippling section and looks at a tall maple tree pulled partway from the ground. Maybe a fox. He picks his way along the edge of the river and stops. Dear God, at his feet lies a baby, stiff and blue with dead round eyes pointing to the sky.

He closes his eyes, feeling another small part of his own life leaving, as if in exchange for the misery of finding a dead baby fallen from the roots of a tree.

He begins to climb, scrambling on his hands and knees, searching for grips among the saplings and large rocks.

He reaches the tree and sits next to it. He looks at the dark space between the embankment and the circular wall of entangled roots, and he wonders, what the hell's in there? He hugs his knees and begins to rock. It's quiet. He stops. Maybe it's not a fox. He rocks again, looking for signs, something to tell him what's in there.

There's nothing.

He leans into the hole and waits for his eyes to adjust to the darkness, and when they do, he sees the outline of a young boy curled up, pressed back to the dark earth and torn roots. He places two heavy fingers on the boy's neck. There's a weak pulse. He leans back, the hard light of the cold day bright against the clear sky.

He stands, slanted on the decline. It's a sign. Time to go. Death is comin again.

He scrambles up the embankment on all fours like some frightened animal having scented danger in the wind. At the top of the embankment, he looks again at the falling tree and he slips away through a strand of young evergreens.

He comes to a road and he finds a dead man next to a horseless wagon. He walks closer. There's a bullet hole in the man's forehead.

He looks to his right, to the slope of the road below him. Two more dead bodies. Both young boys. Both face down on the road.

He turns and walks the road in the other direction and he comes upon two more dead boys. He looks at the valley before him, the long quiet of four hundred acres of shield rock, mixed bush, hardwood, and tall white pine trees. He looks at the Crowe River, winding slow and easy through

the breaking valley floor. He looks at the Gut, a fissure cut into granite, thunderous water, turning and pounding for half a mile.

He walks back toward the falling tree and scrambles down the embankment. He leans into the hole and searches with his hand. He leans farther, his hand finding the back of the boy's shirt, and he drags the boy from the hole.

What were ya doin, hiding? He looks around. I guess ya probably were.

He puts the boy on his chest and he leans back and navigates the sharp decline with his hands and feet.

He stands with the boy over his shoulder, and he walks back the way he'd come. You're heavier than what someone might think. He crosses the river and walks to where the shoreline widens out to a high rocky cliff. There's a large section of tall rock that rumbles out toward the river, and at the crux of this there's a hole in the wall. He crawls into the hole dragging the boy behind him.

The cave opens up higher and he stands. Beyond the damp darkness come the sounds of running water. He lifts the boy and places him on a bed of pine needles covered with the hides of wolves.

The boy sleeps for three days and in that time he dreams. He dreams of hell and he dreams of fear and he dreams of where he lives now and shall forever more. He dreams of the face of horror, the faces of his brothers burning in the long nights of the days before him, and he dreams of this world, of men and blood, with furs and skins and faces painted with the death of others, their hollowed eyes of broken glory coming hard on wild mounts from hell, devil hooves pounding the earth in the name of all that have come before them.

He piles the bodies of the dead in the corner of a rocky field next to the road. And why would he not? For who among us could leave a family there for the ways of this world to pick and chew at without regard for the souls of things? It was the baby that was the hardest to do. Such a thing, one so little and light and lifeless in his arms.

He dragged the first two dead boys up the slope of the road, caught on point, or so it seemed to him: The baby woke and cried and the mother put a waterskin filled with goat's milk to her mouth. She rocked the child and hummed a lullaby, a rifle shot cracking in the quiet morning air and resounding.

The father stood and slapped the reins looking for the boys past the trees that lined the field to the north.

Two more shots.

The wagon approached the bend, his other two sons catching up and riding alongside the wagon. Together they made the turn, the road running straight with a steep decline just before them. They brought their horses to a stop. At the base of the hill, a group of bloodied and battered men, postwar privateers and outlaws with only a few horses among them.

On the downside of the hill, the two boys stretched out dead on the road.

The father watched a man riding west across the field next to them, chasing the boys' horses. He jumped to the ground and lifted his youngest son, Samuel, from the back of the wagon. He looked at his two boys sitting their horses. Ride back to the Gut and lay up somewhere in the valley. He looked back at the men, three of them riding hard up the hill toward them. Go, and he slapped the one horse, the boys turning and riding hard toward the valley.

He watched one of the approaching riders split off from the other two and cut through the field in pursuit of the boys.

He put Samuel on the road next to his mother. The river's that way, and he pointed. Find the embankment and hide. Go, run. Run as fast as you can.

The mother, with the baby in her arms and holding her young son's hand, turned and ran for the woods.

He dragged the father, face down on the flat of the road, dead weighted—the heaviness of nothing in his clenched fist: The father picked his musket up and climbed back onto the wagon. He stood and watched one of the two riders cut away and ride in the direction of his wife and two young children. He sighted his musket, steadying himself, his finger to the trigger, and a bullet ripped into his forehead. He dropped, falling to the ground.

The other two boys he dragged, one at a time, over the dirt road, caught fleeing, so it seemed to him: The boys heard the shot and looked back and turned around again, just in sight of the valley trail. They kicked their horses, the younger of the two lagging behind his older brother.

At a full in-hand gallop the man in pursuit of the boys appeared from the trees and onto the road. The boys looked back, and as they did, the man reached out and grabbed the youngest boy by the collar and threw him to the ground. The older brother reached for his pistol, and as he turned to fire, the man was upon him, slashing a large skinning knife across the boy's throat.

The man rode down the one horse and brought it to a stop. He looked back at the other horse standing over the boy. He rode forward and collected the boy's horse. Before he left, he took his pistol from his belt and shot the boy in the back.

Of the mother he did not find that day, or any other, left to be eaten, gutted and wormed at, her bones chewed and cracked for their marrow, her skull emptied and possibly still there yet: She ran through the woods, thick and heavy with underbrush, her baby in her arms, her youngest son, Samuel, running next to her.

The man in pursuit dismounted and tied his horse to a tree branch. He stood and listened to the sounds of Samuel and his mother stepping on sticks and dried leaves, breaking thin dead tree limbs as they ran. He moved in the direction of their sounds.

They reached the embankment and stopped, the mother peering over the edge. This way. She pulled Samuel along the edge of the embankment. She stopped again and looked down. There, she whispered. That tree hanging by its roots. She looked at Samuel. Sit down.

Samuel sat on the ground and his mother looked behind her. She heard the man approaching. Take Evelyn and go. She put the baby in his arms. Hurry.

What about you?

Shh, she whispered. I'll be right here. I have to watch for the man. She touched his shoulder. Go.

The boy inched forward, the baby in his arms, pressing his feet against the trees below him to brace himself.

The sounds of the man approaching stopped. The mother turned and listened. She looked back and saw Samuel reaching the dark space between the embankment and the tree with half its roots pulled from the ground. She watched the boy and the baby disappear into the dark hole. She turned back to look for the man. She waited, and he broke from the trees.

She screamed and ran away.

And he covered them all with rocks. A roadside grave, moss covered and long forgotten now.

The boy wakes and screams, the old man sitting before a small fire. He says, you're not dead.

The boy backs away like some crab-like cave creature, his hands and feet scrambling amongst the skins and furs of past things and rancid cave dirt until backed against a weeping wall of fear and desolation.

Did you want to say somthin?

All right, well, that's it, that's where I put em. Just so ya know.

He holds out a waterskin. I think this was theirs.

Go on, take it.

They walk without speaking, an old man and a boy, and I watch them go, and I wonder, will he ever dream again, beyond these cold breaths of time that have him now?

And the question settles upon him.

Stay close.

In the shadows of the wall.

We'll see em first if they ever come again.

Let's sit and drink some of this cold river water. It's quiet enough, don't you think, boy?

Put the sun there.

He puts the sun there.

Pass me that. He rinses his mouth and spits. I almost didn't do it, if you want to know the truth. And you know why? He takes another drink. Cause nothin can ever change without changing another thing. He wipes his mouth with the back of his hand and holds the waterskin back out to the boy. Here, damnit, you do it. And who among us can ever say the one thing is on the side of a good thing? Who? And that's just the way it is, boy. The way it is, and always will be.

That ever-lovin warmin sun sure feels nice, though, doesn't it?

It'll be a long winter, a hard winter, you'll see. Lord knows how I made it through that first one? Misery and death everywhere. But it wouldn't come for me.

No.

I did more than just wish, though, didn't I?

Did.

It's harder than what ya might first think. I had a hard time of it. Failed miserably.

In the cold.

Takes a lot of strength.

In the dark.

A lot of will.

Did I mention I have a sister? Lots of gardens and sunshine where she lives, and we could go there, if we wanted to.

He lifts his head. Are you sleepin? I guess you probably are.

He puts his head back down. I suppose that's what I'm trying to say, boy, we could try if we wanted to.

On the road at night, by the stars—all the living stars. Just you and me.

And by the river, by the trees, beneath the ever-lovin warmin sun, the old man's words drift away with the cold river water, and a little breeze comes too.

Haunted we can become. Events so tragic we relive them, over and over.

Over and over.

He's an old man standing in a river. He hears a sound. He looks toward a fallen tree. Maybe a fox. He crosses the river and stops. Dear God, at his feet lies a baby, stiff and blue with dead round eyes pointing to the sky.

BLOOD-RED ON THE BAY

A dead crow's nest hangs falling before the coming night, a simple silhouette to a barren land.

A wind picks up and takes the nest and it drifts crazy-like above the road—so far now from that little bay of Bala, hands laid upon the water. And I am coming.

The nest breaks apart and flutters away and she walks away, slow and unsure, so beautiful, thin and broken—perfect really, for this movement, wandering and wondering, in a big world.

The wind pushing her on, and now down a narrow path between tall trees born of the coming night's broken light—most of wanting is always there, in the trees without leaves, in the wind: You can't have everything. You can't fix everything.

She stops and picks a small white spotted mushroom. She sniffs it. She puts her tongue to it. She gives it back to the wet ferns, white trilliums, and broken punky trees.

She starts up the small ditch back to the path.

There's an old woman, dressed in black, walking with her head held forward, pushing a wooden cart filled with assorted possessions the other way on the other side of the path. A raven rides proud on point.

She watches the old woman walking with her heavy labored shuffle, one foot up with slow deliberation and put down again firm in front of the other.

The old woman stops and looks back. Go on then, what'ya waitin for?

She walks again, the sun falling over the trees, and she stops and turns to it, tilting her head back, closing her eyes, and she stays like this, on this path to where? That postcard. Faded. Pinned to the wall at the back of the diner where she worked. You didn't even know who sent it, they'd left before you started.

The water in the postcard, so calm and clear and running on forever, and there were no clouds, in a clear blue sky. None at all.

So beautiful and peaceful and filled with such loneliness.

Against the building, white siding, the paint mostly faded and flaked away, the sun setting on the bay, he fucked you.

Yes.

The path comes to an end, and there's a rocky, craggy drop, and beyond it, it is stunning. She starts down the slope, looking on, listening—there's a breeze, and she walks to it, reaching to it, the long soft grass brushing against her, the sun hard upon it, soft and warm, and she walks like this, in the endless valley meadow, until sometime later when she tires and stretches back to the warmth of the tall grass.

I had a child.

Yes.

The child died.

She stares at the clear blue sky, and there are no clouds. None at all. She drifts to sleep, the breeze carrying to her the remembrance of the smell of her new child.

She wakes shaded by a big tree. A beautiful tree. Perfectly formed and reaching far above her.

She backs away, and in her mind she is unsure of the tree, questioning the very thing before her. The existence of the tree. Such a beautiful tree. She looks beyond it, and there is something. She can't make it out. It's too far, the sun low and setting in her eyes and she begins to walk again, looking back at the tree to see if it's really there. Still there. Such a thing as that.

I was working.

Your father alone with the baby.

Yes, babysitting.

A learned man, a man of words.

He read his Bible. It is written: I should be loyal to the nightmare of my choice, and that's you, you little slut, and he beat her.

Bloodied her.

He did more than just that.

Yes.

Late at night drunk on the floor he'd quote Conrad: "And this stillness of life did not in the least resemble a peace. It was the stillness of an implacable force brooding over an inscrutable intention. It looked at you with a vengeful aspect."

She comes to a caravan-type trailer, wooden with trim painted in faded bright colors, the grass up past the door, the wheels taken by the earth.

She looks around. There's no one.

The father of your baby finished high school. You didn't.

No, I had the baby.

He fled Bala and he fled the memories of you—of his fucking, and he fled too, the memory of your dead baby.

Yes.

She sits on the trailer hitch perched on a block of cracked aged oak, the sun falling upon her, upon her suffering—her hollowing; and with tears in her eyes, she lifts her face to it, the good warmth of it, the words within it.

I have a friend.

I know, baby.

She lives in a tree.

That's right.

I'm going to close my eyes. Did you kiss me?

Yes, baby, on your forehead.

On my forehead?

Yes.

I love you.

I know, baby, I love you too.

Hello?

There's a man.

I didn't mean to—and she wipes the tears from her eyes.

Overhear them? That's all right. He pushes back his sweat-stained straw trilby and reaches into his pocket for his cigarettes.

Where'd you come from?

He looks over his shoulder, his white shirt tucked in at the front hangs loose at the back. I live here.

You do?

Yes, and he lights his cigarette and flips shut his lighter and nods toward the trailer.

She looks back at the trailer and sees the markings of faded painted letters—Circus.

He pulls a pint of whiskey from his suit jacket pocket and unscrews the top and holds it out to her.

No, thank you. You were in the circus?

Yes, and he tips back the bottle. A clown. The sad one.

A sad clown?

Yeah, you know, with the makeup.

You're a little girl?

She looks back at the trailer.

And now another voice comes, yes, I'm a little girl, and this voice, it drifts just above the tall grass, under the fading of the light. I live in the tree.

With my friend?

No, I am your friend.

Oh, I see, you're a little girl?

32

Yes, I'm a little girl.

Am I a little girl?

Yes, you're a little girl too.

The sad clown places his foot on the hitch. So, you didn't tell me, where are you from?

Far away.

That doesn't help much.

Bala. What was that?

Bala?

Yes, Bala. It's a little place on a bay. Are you gonna tell me or not?

He takes another sip of whiskey and looks at the trailer.

In the tree you don't look little.

No, I'm not always little.

In my dreams, I see you, and I climb you, and you hold me.

Yes.

You keep me.

Yes.

Can we play?

Yes. Come and play.

In the tree?

Yes. Come and play in the tree with me.

You won't make me leave?

No.

Is it warm?

Yes, it's warm. It's nice.

She looks back at the sad clown. It's like we can hear her dream somehow? Is that it? Both sides of it?

He screws the lid on the bottle and puts it back in his suit jacket pocket and sits on the hitch. Either that or we are her dream. But then again, I wouldn't know, would I? I was born here. Tell me about this place, Bala? Why'd you leave?

I don't know.

He crosses his legs and lights another cigarette. You don't know?

No. Well—there was a postcard.

A postcard?

At the back of the diner where I worked. It was old and faded and sent by someone that left before I started. On my break I'd look at it and wish I was there. All the time, actually. I'd even touch it.

He takes a drag of his cigarette. So you wanted to leave?

I guess so, although—

He drops his wrist over his crossed legs, his cigarette burning down between his fingers. Yes?

Nothing.

Nothing?

No.

No? He takes another drag of his cigarette and looks back at the trailer.

Baby, the lions are stuck.

The lions?

Yes, baby, the lions. I need Kashka to pull the truck out.

Kashka?

Yes, baby, Kashka.

It's sunny.

Yes, it is. It's sunny.

It's so warm.

Yes, it's nice. You look beautiful.

Where're the midgets?

Midgets?

Yes.

Gone.

Gone?

Yes, baby, gone. In the mud.

There's just the lions left?

Yes. And us.

Us?

Yes, baby. Everything else is in the mud.

And Kashka?

No, not Kashka.

Look. The lions.

Oh?

Yes, I see them.

Yes, I see them now too.

They're running and playing, like that time on the beach, do you remember? Just them. In the meadow now, and they look so happy.

Yes, baby, they are. They're happy.

What about the truck?

It's gone now too. In the mud.

I can see the tree from here. I think I'll go see if my friend wants to come out and play. She might want to come for a ride on Kashka?

That would be nice.

Yes, it would. What will you do?

Me?

Yes.

Wait.

Wait?

Yes, baby, wait.

For the others?

Yes, for the others. They might come back.

Did you kiss me?

No, you're on Kashka.

Blow me a kiss.

There. Did you get it?

Yes, on my forehead. I love you.

I know, baby, I love you too.

Where is this place?

Here?

Yes.

The end of the world, of course.

It is?

Yes.

Who are those people? And why am I here?

Perhaps to find me. Tell me more about that night.

She looks at the last of the sun on the tall grass. I was on my break and I walked to the water's edge. It was such a beautiful night, a warm breeze coming off the bay, the sun setting, and I wanted to hear the music.

Music?

Yes, there's a big club at the other end of the bay and Louis Armstrong was playing.

He tilts his head back and exhales. Louis Armstrong.

The bay was full, there were so many boats that night, all moored together, their varnished wood shining just above the water, the women in their long dresses and jewelry holding their high heels in one hand and their husbands' arm with the other, walking barefoot across the bows of the boats. And for some reason, I wanted to feel the water. I can't remember why.

You wanted your child?

Yes, I wanted my child. I knelt down and leaned forward and put my hands to it, both palms, and it made me feel good, as if I were connected somehow to all of it, the warm breeze, the water, the boats gently swaying, the sun setting and all the happy people. And of course, the music, that beautiful music that just seemed to cover us, to fold us all into one thing, into everything, and time could have stopped right there, for all I cared. She looks at the soft yellow light coming from the trailer window. And I can feel it still, as if it'll be with me forever.

The sad clown butts his cigarette out against the side of the hitch and looks at the trailer.

You're an old woman?

Yes, I'm an old woman.

Am I an old woman?

Yes, you're an old woman too.

I've been riding this elephant.

Yes, I know.

I wanted to see if you wanted to come for a ride? I was going to ask you?

That would be nice.

You'd like to come for a ride?

Yes.

Where would you like to go?

It doesn't matter.

No?

No.

What about the tree?

It's with me.

The tree?

Yes, the tree.

Do you like being a little girl, with a tree?

Riding an elephant?

Yes, riding an elephant.

Yes.

The sad clown stands and holds his hand out and she takes it, and together they walk into the endless valley meadow, and there are no clouds in a clear blue sky. None at all. The sun setting, blood-red on the bay above her.

QUIET IN THE DARK

In a dark paneled room without windows, the man ran the trains. Two big chandeliers reflecting a dimmed light sparkling down the will of his control. He ran the trains over long Parker truss bridges, through the towns, around the bends, and over green fields. He ran the trains through the station, past the people, and high over the hills too.

Look at em go, shiny and go. Round and round. He put the box down, his big cigar between his big fingers, and he dimmed the lights more.

He sat back in his big chair and watched the trains go. Slow and steady. Slow and steady now. His heavy crystal glass in his hand and he put it all back. He blew more big smoke over the big train world. The trains moving on. He poured more whiskey and he smoked more. His dark eyes in a dark world watching the trains go. A slow train coming. Save our cities—no. Save our souls—no. The future is certain. The trains moving on—the end shall never come. He sat forward and drank more, he smoked more, his eyes fixed upon the trains—look at em go, shiny and go. Round and round.

He took the big cigar from his mouth and he reached out and jabbed the air, that burn, that sting. He jabbed again and he yelled, where is Papa? Louder in the dark, the trains moving on.

Where is Papa at? Tell me. Tell me now. And he jabbed harder and he screamed louder, where the fuck is Papa now?

And then, quiet in the dark, the trains moving on, like the spoken single keys of a refrain: Come, break me. Do it now.

And this man, one of the last kings, stood in the dark, a light he had dimmed himself, and he stepped forward and shut the trains down, and the silence that came was like a rattle and hum, like the piled and broken bones of all of us against the coming winds of our certainties. Of knowing itself.

And like a lamp held high in daylight, we must secure the existence of our people and a future for our children. Must we not?

He closed the door and the trains ran on. Look at em go, shiny and go. Round and round.

IN A SMALL TOWN
(CALLED AMERICA)

It's getting worse, and Jake finished his beer, and together they listened to the rain on the tin roof of the drive-shed. The receptiveness of its falling. The comfort within its echoing.

And he said, things are lookin up.

Damn straight, said Jared.

I mean, now that things are great again, things are lookin up, and Jake stood and walked to the fridge and grabbed two more beers. He passed one to Jared and sat back down on the block of cracked white oak. He took a sip and looked at his younger brother. I went and saw the doc.

Oh?

Said I'm shooting blanks.

Shit, Jake. I'm sorry to hear that. Have ya told Sugar?

Last night.

How'd that go?

'Bout as good as you'd think. Ya know how much she wants kids. Not that I don't—I mean, you got your two and they're doin okay, right?

Right.

Thing is, I don't wanna adopt some stranger's baby and say it's mine. Sugar don't neither. We could get her artificially knocked up, but—

41

What?

Jake shrugged and took another sip.

They got DNA.

I know they got DNA, but nothin's perfect, and it might work out you're paying for somethin a little less than what you'd hoped for, ya know what I mean?

I guess.

And then you're just fucked.

So what'ya thinkin?

Well ... and Jake paused, thinking for a moment. I want you to do it.

You what?

You heard me.

Are you askin me to fuck Sugar?

Yup.

Really?

Yup.

Have you lost your goddamn mind?

Jake lifted his John Deere ball cap, scratched the top of his balding head, and said, nope.

Does Sugar know?

We talked about it.

You talked about it?

Yup.

And what'ya think, Alice is gonna be okay with me walkin next door and havin a go with Sugar? Cause I got news for ya, she won't be.

She don't gotta know.

What'ya mean she don't gotta know? How the hell is she not gonna know?

Cause we ain't gonna tell her, that's how.

For fuck's sake, this is nuts, I can't fuck Sugar.

What'ya mean you can't fuck Sugar? She looks good still. Hell, she's a lot better lookin than that girl you were fuckin back in high school.

She wasn't that bad.

The hell she wasn't.

C'mon, Jake, get serious, you don't mean this shit?

I'm as serious as the day is long, little brother. Hell, it won't take more than a time or two. Didn't ya always tell me all you had to do to knock up Alice was to hang your pants on the bed post?

True enough, but still—.

At least this way the kid'll be a Burleson. Jake finished his beer and threw the empty at the garbage can. Besides, ya don't gotta worry 'bout a thing. We'll just get up a little early, you walk to my place, and I'll come here. After you're done, you come back here like nothing ever happened, and I'll head back home. Jake stood. Just think about it. He walked to the door and looked back. Oh, and by the way, Sugar says she'll be droppin eggs in the next day or two.

She'll be what?

That's what she said.

You talked about it?

Yup, we talked about it. Later.

Yeah, said Jared. Fuck me.

Jake opened the door and walked to the fridge and grabbed a beer. How'd it go?

Standing at the workbench cleaning an engine part Jared looked back.

Ya got it done, right?

Yeah, I got it done, but I had to turn her around.

What? Why? She looks good still.

No, I mean, to do it, ya know.

I guess, and Jake tipped back his beer.

Maybe cause she's your wife, or somethin like that, what'ya think?

How long ya been married?

Eleven years.

Do ya love her still?

What? Yeah, I guess. How the hell am I supposed to know?

It's hard to know, ain't it?

Yeah, it's not easy.

Ya think she still loves you?

Of course she does. Why wouldn't she?

I didn't say she didn't. What about Sugar?

What about her?

Think she still loves me?

Hell, I don't know. Why?

It's just something ya wonder about, ya know? That's all. It's not like it's not possible. It happens all the time.

I guess.

Do ya think it matters?

What?

Love.

I don't know—for fuck's sake, Jake.

Jake tossed his empty at the garbage can. I think it does. He walked to the door and looked back. We'd best try again tomorrow, while things are goin good that way.

Goin good?

Yeah, said Jake. See ya.

Yeah, said Jared. Later.

Sugar walked out the door, her flip-flops smacking her heels, her white short dress tight all the way down.

She crossed the adjoining properties and reached the gravel driveway. She looked away, somewhere, and took a drag of her cigarette. She tossed it to the gravel and toed it out and she opened the drive-shed door.

Her eyes adjusting to the dim light she walked to the fridge and grabbed a beer. She looked at the calendar hanging on the wall, some girl with less than little on draped over the hood of a shiny red car. They make good money, ya know. She opened the beer and looked back at the poster. A blonde, like her. It's not just the money, it's the connections. Ya know that, right?

She walked to the workbench and pulled herself onto a high metal stool. She crossed her legs, her one foot bouncing—a nervous energy of how she was hinged, much like this place itself. I suppose ya talked about it?

Not much we did, no.

She took a sip of beer and leaned back, her thin milky-white forearms resting on the workbench, her dress high up on her long legs, and she tilted her head, the thickness of her blonde hair falling to one side and catching the light, just right, and she knew it, and did so without having to. What'd he say? She looked at her chipped red nail polish.

He wanted to know if it went okay.

And?

And what?

What'ya say?

Not much.

Not much?

No. Can we not talk about this?

Why don't ya wanna talk about it?

What's the point?

The point? She uncrossed her legs and crossed them the other way, her foot starting to bounce. Why's it gotta be so hot in here? What's wrong with that damn fan? She leaned forward. The point is, we need to figure this out, and right this goddamn minute we do.

Jared grabbed a rag and began to wipe his hands. What's with you?

Did ya not hear us last night? I'd be surprised if ya didn't.

A little, I did. What was up? He walked to the fridge and grabbed a beer.

I told him, I ain't no puppy-mill slut, and I ain't sleeping with you no more.

Jared stopped. You're what?

What?

They looked at one another.

You ain't sleeping with me no more?

Of course I am, I just ain't doin it for him no more.

That makes no sense.

Are you dumb? There's a world of difference between my wanting to sleep with you and him wanting me to. And I can tell you this much, we had better figure this out, and I mean now.

Jared leaned against the bench and sipped his beer. How long we been together?

I don't know, a couple of years. Why?

In all that time we been doin it, were ya never worried about getting pregnant? Or were ya just hoping ya would and say it was Jake's?

Ya don't get it, do you? All this damn talk of babies, I can hardly take it.

What'ya mean?

She put her beer down and got up and began to pace in her flip-flops. It's the last thing I'm ever gonna do, do ya understand that?

What?

This world is a hard world, Jared Burleson, and it gets no easier being a woman, that's for damn sure. She picked up her beer and took a sip. And if you think I'm gonna get dropped down another rung or two by having either yours or your brother's damn babies, ya gotta another thing comin. Besides, it plays absolute havoc with your body, destroys it completely. She looked at Jared. Is that what you want?

Hold on, Sugar, are you telling me all this time you've been on birth control?

That is correct, smart boy, yes I have.

And all this time Jake thought you were trying to get pregnant?

Correct.

And then it turns out, he's sterile? What would ya have done if he hadn't been?

I don't know. I'd of figured somethin out.

And now he's got me doin ya to get ya pregnant even though I already am and you're on birth control?

She pulled herself back up onto the stool. As it turns out, yes. She took a sip of beer.

Jared pushed off the workbench and stood in front of Sugar, his hands reaching past her to the workbench. You're somethin, Sugar. I don't know what, but you're definitely somethin.

The small fan in the window began to rattle and it blew warm sticky air.

Sweat from his forehead dropped to her thigh.

She looked at her leg, at the drop, and she put her finger to it, and it ran like a tear.

She felt the smooth touch of her dress, moving up, and she pushed herself forward on the stool, just a little, just enough, a lazy southern cat stretching its underbelly to the warming sun.

Sugar.

I know, baby, and she put her arms around his neck and she looked out the small window. At the scrubby land. At the coming heat. A small bird came to the window. Maybe a starling? She didn't know. She did once, when she was just a little girl.

A ROADSIDE LUNCH

Hey.

Jonathan stopped and looked.

Ya want some lunch?

He was unsure if the woman in the field was speaking to him. He looked around to see if there was anyone else.

She laughed. Ya, you. Who else would I be talkin to? Come on, I got plenty.

He sat the horse.

Come on, already, I won't bite.

He rode down and up the wide ditch and onto the grassy field. He stopped and looked down at the woman. She had long, thick auburn hair and freckles, a long print summer dress over white thermal long Johns, thick grey socks pulled up past her brown leather hiking boots. Over the top of the dress she had a thick grey sweater. Hanging from a wide brown leather belt were a half dozen or so snake skins. She held a hunting knife with a wide blade.

That's a nice horse.

Thanks.

What's her name?

Destiny.

Destiny? That's a good name, I like it. Come on down, lunch is about ready.

Jonathan dismounted. He wrapped the reins around the pommel of the saddle and backed the girth strap off and let Destiny graze the tall field grass.

The woman pointed her knife toward the blanket spread out on the grass next to a campfire where something was cooking in a small cast-iron frying pan. Have a seat. On the blanket was a sawed-off shotgun, a pair of binoculars, a bottle of wine, a wine glass, and a plate.

Goodness me, where are my manners. She extended her hand. My name's Priscilla, although my daddy always called me, Miss Lady Grey, but Priscilla's fine.

He shook her hand. Jonathan.

Pleased to meet you, Jonathan. Have a seat.

He took his shotgun off and sat and placed the gun on the blanket. Priscilla squatted next to the fire and tended to the cooking strips of meat, onions, and peppers. Here, have a glass of wine. It's French. She poured a glass and handed it to Jonathan. Here's to company. She held up the bottle.

They toasted one another and took a sip.

So why did ya?

Why'd I what? Ask ya to lunch?

Yeah.

I dunno, I had my glasses on ya. She nodded toward the binoculars. And ya seemed nice enough. Besides, I'm celebratin and felt like some company, and there you were, just like that, plain as day, riding a horse. And I can tell ya what, it's not every day you see that, now is it?

What'ya celebrating?

It's my last day on the job. She used her hunting knife to mix the food in the frying pan. That's getting a little too hot, and she set the frying pan on the edge of the fire.

Doing what?

Huntin snakes, of course.

Snakes?

Yup. She shook the skins attached to her belt. They're worth a fortune.

Snake skins?

Oh yeah, they use em for lots of things, boots, wallets, purses, you name it. Especially these big black rat snakes. She shook a couple of the large black and copper skins. They grow big, which is good, up to five or six feet, even bigger, if ya get lucky. She grabbed the cloth next to the fire and picked up the frying pan and scooped out a portion onto the plate. She put the pan back on the edge of the fire and passed the plate to Jonathan.

Thanks.

My pleasure. You got your own knife, I suppose.

Jonathan unsheathed his knife and scooped a mouthful.

Makes a nice little meal, don't it?

Jonathan stopped chewing and pointed his knife at the snake skin hanging from her belt.

Priscilla laughed. What'ya think it was? Chicken?

Jonathan swallowed the food and took a sip of wine.

She smiled. You're somethin, I dunno what, but you're definitely somethin. I could set ya up in business, if ya wanted to. I'm quittin anyway. What'ya say? Ya interested?

Thanks, but we have a farm.

Oh? Where's that?

New Acadia.

Would you look at that, I don't even know where that is. Am I not the most ignorant thing you ever met? But I'm sure it's nice. What kinda farm is it?

Mostly sheep.

Too bad. You can make a killin doin this.

So why you quitting?

I'm goin to Paris.

France?

Yup, I'm gonna travel. See some civilization. I deserve it after huntin snakes in these godforsaken woods for the last ten years. Hell, there ain't a single day I haven't thought about it. Over and over like a broken record. And now I'm goin. I got pretty much every dollar I ever made chasin these limbless little bastards and it ain't a day too soon, neither, I can tell ya that. I was goin crazy, certifiable lock me up crazy. Worse than that even, I'd of killed somebody, maybe even my own self. I kid you not. A person can only take so many days livin with an itch they can't scratch. You know what I mean? Probably ya don't, but ya can trust me on that. I know all about itches, more than I ever thought I'd wanna know, that's for damn sure. There's types of itches ya can't scratch that will slowly drive you crazy, and I mean the very worst kinda crazy, silent and nuttier than hell in your head type crazy, the kind that builds and builds and won't stop buildin until the next thing ya know you're chasin butterflies through a fire. And then there's the kind you can scratch, but of course, those are the ones you don't wanna have to scratch, leastways, not by your own self. Funny how life works that way, ain't it? Here, have some more wine and let's forget about our troubles. Leastways for a little while. She filled his glass and took another sip from the bottle.

Jonathan took another sip and looked at Priscilla. Do you have any family that could take your work over?

Nope. I did, but my father died when I was just young. I didn't know my mom. I had a husband once. But he's dead now too.

I'm sorry.

Don't be, it was some time ago. Besides, he was nothin but a snake in the grass himself. My husband that is. My father was a prince of a man. What about you?

There's just me and my mom, but she's missing.

Oh? I'm sorry to hear that. How long has she been gone?

Couple of days.

Is that what you doin, lookin for her?

Jonathan nodded and took another sip.

How come you're riding a horse?

Our truck was stolen.

Someone stole your truck?

Yup.

When did it go missin, the same time as your mom?

Nope, afterward.

So your mom went missin, then your truck went missin?

Yeah.

D'ya think someone did something to her, then took the truck?

I think so.

Well, I hope you find her. I really do. And I hope she's all right.

Thanks.

She topped up Jonathan's glass and tipped back the bottle. She put the bottle down and picked up Jonathan's plate and put it in the frying pan and stood. Finish your wine and relax, I'm just gonna give these a quick rinse in the creek down there.

I can help, and he started to stand.

No, that's all right. It'll just take a minute. Sit and enjoy the sunshine. Lord knows we don't get much of it. She began to leave. She stopped and looked back. Ya think ya might've been better off trying to find her first? That way you'd know what happened?

I thought about it, but by then it would've been too late and they'd be gone.

She looked as if she might say something more but didn't. I'll be right back.

Destiny lifted her head and watched Priscilla walking by.

Jonathan stretched out on the blanket, taking the warmth of the sun to his face, and he closed his eyes.

He opened his eyes. Priscilla was there, standing before him.

I changed my mind. She placed the dishes on the ground and sat and unlaced her boots.

Jonathan sat up.

Why should I waste all that good wine and this fine sunshine doin dishes? She slipped her boots and socks off and stood and pulled her heavy sweater over her head. She undid her belt, with the snakeskins hanging from it, and dropped it to the ground. She pulled her dress over her head and stood in her small pair of white panties, a silver chain with a silver snake head hanging around her neck. I told ya, I was celebratin, didn't I? What are ya waitin for? Take your coat off.

Jonathan didn't move, still just staring at Priscilla.

She laughed and walked forward and straddled him. Here, let me help ya.

She took his coat off and undid his shirt. She undid his belt and she pushed him onto his back—desire. All of it. The cold loneliness of unfulfillment seeking the scent and strength of his young body. Together, succumbing to the flooding of pleasure.

She walked barefoot to the river carrying the dishes, just her dress on, the snake skins hanging at her side.

Destiny still grazing, watched her walk by again.

What a fine day this turned out to be, horse, wouldn't ya say?

She washed the dishes and placed them on the grassy riverbank. She stood and looked at the river. She looked at the bridge, and she walked along the shallow shoreline, and she walked across the tall field grass to the road, and walked up the road to the bridge and stopped in the middle of it. She untied two long rat snake skins from her belt and she tied them together. She tied one end to the bridge railing and she fastened a noose at the other end. She stepped over the railing and stood on the ledge. She placed the noose over her head and tightened it, and without saying a word, she jumped, the tied rat snake skins breaking, the running river water taking her away.

UNDER THE MIDNIGHT SUN

Oh fuck no, and he'll lift his head from a thick and darkening pool of his own blood. Hellish pain rushing forward. Dirt and gravel stuck to the side of his face.

RVs driving by, a long line of em.

He'll puke, mostly blood, and he'll look up, a long dribble of spit and blood hanging from his lower lip. He'll see a man with dark hair driving by, a woman with long black hair sitting next to him, a young girl and a young boy in the back.

Oh Momma, look, the young girl will say.

The woman will look and Finn'll see the woman's beautiful blue eyes.

Don't look, her mother will tell her.

But Momma.

Tell her, the dad'll say.

I did.

But Momma.

Don't look, her momma will say again.

He'd like to stand, but he can't. He'd like the RVs to stop, but they won't.

A pickup will come, pulling off the road, a young kid with long dark hair stepping out and walking to the back of it.

You got something to smoke?

You mean like—.

Yeah.

Right here and ready to go. The kid'll fire up a joint and take a pull. He'll hold the smoke. He'll exhale. Dude, you look totally fucked up. He'll step forward and pass the joint.

The man'll close his eyes and inhale.

The kid'll look back at the big lights of the big town. Poor fucker, I wonder what the deal is? He'll look back at Finn. I'd take you back there, but I can't. I don't got the time.

You got something to drink?

I gotta couple of beers in the truck, ya want one?

Yeah, and Finn'll take another hit. He'll open his eyes and the kid'll be there standing before him with a cold can of beer. Thanks. He'll open it and tip it back and try to swallow and it'll hurt like hell. He'll lower the beer and take a last hit of the joint and drop the thin stained nub of rolling paper to the ground. You need to be careful.

What the fuck are you talkin about?

A road like this can be dangerous.

Whatever, dude.

I'm just sayin, and he'll watch the kid get back in the truck and start it up and wait to cut back into the long line of RVs.

He'll manage to stand, bracing himself against the rushing air of the passing RVs, the front of his white shirt ruffling in the moving air, the back soaked with blood. He'll tilt his head back and close his eyes to feel the wind on his face, and his equilibrium will drop out and he'll fall.

In the back pocket of his jeans his phone'll vibrate.

He'll try to sit and won't be able to and so he'll dig his left hand into the dirt for a purchase by which to pull himself up, dragging his feet over the ground, leaning forward, resting his arms on his knees.

His breathing, slow and thin.

His heart racing.

He'll try to stand and won't be able to, draining the last of his strength, increasing the pounding pain in his head. Closing his eyes he'll quiet himself, and in his mind all he'll be able to see are the RVs stretching out on the road as far as his mind can see.

Everythin all right?

He'll look up and see an older man with long grey hair tied in a ponytail turning his motorcycle off and setting the kickstand.

Anything I can do?

Finn'll try and speak.

I think your phone is ringing, can you get it? Where's it at? In your pocket?

It'll vibrate again and the man'll walk around to the back of Finn and before he can reach into Finn's pocket he'll see a fresh line of blood trickling out of a small hole in the back of Finn's head, just below his skull and to the right of his spine, pushing out past darkened blood mixed with bits of dirt and gravel. Fuck me, would you look at that. He'll see a gun on the road. Ya really fucked this up, didn't ya? He'll take the phone from Finn's pocket. It'll vibrate. Do you want it?

Finn'll look at the phone and fall from the heels of his boots.

The biker will catch him and help him sit upright. Jesus Christ, you're just about stone cold dead, aren't ya? He'll look at the phone and back at Finn. Can you hear me? Are you still there? I think it's your kids.

He'd like to stand.

What'ya want me to do?

But he can't.

It's from Mackenzie. Would ya like me to read it to ya?

He'd like the RVs to stop.

She says, hey Dad, Cael's with me, we're here for the call. Dad? Are you there?

But they won't.

She wants to know if you're still coming home for her graduation, she says, it's in two weeks.

The phone'll vibrate and the biker will look again and he'll pause, not wanting to read anymore, not wanting anymore of these shitty reminders of how life can be, and he'll place the phone on Finn's lap. It's there if you want it.

The biker will stand. I'll tell ya what, I'll call 911, but that's it, that's all I can do. They won't get here for a while, but at least you won't be left out here dead on the side of the road.

He'll get back on his bike and take his phone from his jacket pocket and make the call. He'll give his name and the reason for his call and hang up. He'll put his phone away and look back at Finn. Listen, brother, I'm sorry about your troubles, I really am, but I gotta go. He'll start the bike up and take it off the kickstand and ride down the side of the road, tucking in behind an RV, disappearing back into the long line of their conformity that rolls on over these high hills without trees in perfect sync and harmony until fading away somewhere just beyond the farthest reaches of the midnight sun.

A gunshot.

An old man riding a horse stops.
A wolf trailing him stops.
The man rides on, the wolf following.

They come upon the fallen man, the old man stopping his horse, the wolf stretching out in the tall grass next to the road, resting its head on its front paws, watching the old man dismount.

He approaches Finn and bends to one knee, placing two fingers on Finn's neck. Yes yes, I see.

The wolf closes its eyes.

The old man begins searching through the man's pockets. He looks in the direction of the gun on the road, the old man's eyes mostly milky white and nothing more. He opens the backpack next to the man and begins to search through it, and as he does, he begins to speak: When I was just a boy, we moved to a little nothing of a farm. And it was, it wasn't much at all. You'd ride up that long laneway, cross a creek, and dog leg left to get to the house. And where that laneway bent, he uses his right hand to illustrate a dog leg left, there was a slaughterhouse, on the outside of the turn, for horses. Pitiful. Flies everywhere. He holds his hands up before him and indicates a space of about a foot and a half. Rats this big. It was terrible, all those horse carcasses piled up, one on top of the other, 'till you'd think the wagon was about to tip over. Headless and skinned, butchered with their hooves still on. 'Course as soon as we moved there my father wouldn't have anything to do with it, bein how he was into horses. He was a trainer, one of the very best.

He stands and reaches his hand out and strokes the side of the horse's head. Well, of course, he tore that slaughterhouse down, cleared everything away, like you'd never know it was ever there. New sod and everything.

He looks up the long, quiet road. Nothing moving. No wind. A perfect silence. He looks back at Finn. We had this big pasture to the front of the house, and my father, he'd tell me to go fetch such and such a horse, and I would, running down that long laneway, fetching the horse out of the pasture. And every single time, and I do mean every time, with any horse, over all the years I lived and worked there, I'd walk a horse up that beautiful laneway with the big willows hangin over it, well, just as soon as I'd start around that dog leg, all hell would break loose. They'd spook, rearin up and steppin back. Now why would that be? Why would a horse, years and years after we'd tore that slaughterhouse down, spook, in that very spot? Every time? Every horse?

He pauses, stroking the side of the horse's head. Just think, if you were a horse, what that place must have seemed like?

He mounts his horse and looks back toward Finn. I've often wondered, what if some people were like that? If they too could see beyond what was just there? And if they could, what kinda of darkness that would be? Even just a glimpse, you would think, would be enough.

He kicks the horse and starts up the road. Imagine, he says, a look into the slaughterhouse of all man's time. Yes yes, just horrible. An unimaginable darkness.

The wolf lifts its head and watches the old man riding away. It stands and approaches the fallen man. Looking around, it lowers its head and sniffs the man. And then as if satisfied with what it has found, it crouches and leaps and begins to run, following the old man up the road, over these high rolling hills without trees, disappearing somewhere just beyond the farthest reaches of the midnight sun.

ON THE PRAIRIE, WEST
OF THE THIRD MERIDIAN

I'll admit, what I did was rather unusual—at least for others to try to understand. Not that I considered it to be any of their business.

Me? No, I never doubted it, not once, despite everything that happened, how it ended, my living here—forced to be living here, and now, mercifully, having died here.

A broken man.

A fallen man.

But he wasn't always.

And this man, does he dream still? Of a place, of a time, these dreams of his long prairie nights.

He stands upon the land and picks locusts from his hair and from his beard that are not there now. The air tight this day with the sharp edge of prairie cold. The sky closed. He looks.

Blue and red lights. Blue and red lights.

By the road.

The long road.

The Number Two road.

Betrayed by what?

He does not know.

Men in suits, heavy coats, and fur hats. Their faces red. Their words cold in the air before them.

Tom?

The river is there.

It's fifteen mile yet.

He looks at the men. I walked.

You what, Tom?

He points, his hand-sewn canvas coat stiff with cold. South. Six hundred miles.

Crawling from the darkness and wanting more you stood that line, and they beat you, and they beat you bad. Isn't that right, Tom?

They'll be no unions, not here, not on the Iron Range, there won't.

Your house on fire.

Your daughter—.

Scarred for life.

All four of your children taken and placed in foster homes.

Your wife dead from influenza.

Locked away—insane. At least, that's what they said.

And you were jailed.

But you found your boy, though, didn't you?

You take him in the night. The cold Minnesota night, and you walk, six hundred miles, and at the border, they take him again.

I shall come again.

The boy waits. By the window. By the door.

And you do come again, and together you walk six hundred more miles, the uncertainty of the journey there before you both.

They take him, and you're deported. You'll be arrested if you try again.

And so you farm, south of Moose Jaw, west of the third meridian.

You look at the large willow rollers linked with heavy chain. Frozen. The white of the horse's ribs just above the drifting snow and you put your blackened fingers to the frost of your beard and search for what is not there now.

Madness.

He should've been off this land years ago.

They say, he'd walk seven miles with three hundred pounds of supplies on his back.

That's what they say.

Hell of a man.

And you remember, you made a thresher you shared with your neighbors, a tricycle you peddled with your hands, a clock powered by water, special pliers to pull your teeth out, the new ones forged by you.

You look at the rollers, your fingers crawling, and you look to the river—the only river, and you point there, for it shall carry you away, back to the fold, back to the rhythm from which you fell so very long ago.

You build a fiddle and play in the night, this music of your dreams, of the sea and of the wind, time screaming loneliness, your children, too, pushing you on, for this man shall sail away, alone on his prairie nights.

And then, Tom?

All the world died.

The drought killing the land, the locusts coming that plague you still. Your neighbors lost their homes—lost their farms, this impractical obsession of yours growing from the dust of their broken dreams.

Some stayed.

Some left.

Others come, in trucks, by foot, and some riding rails, but not you, for you shall sail away.

You build your forge up and on you go, rolls of metal and rolls of steel and long sheets of iron too.

A hand upon your shoulder. A broad shoulder. In the cold. Don't you worry, Tom, we'll take good care of her.

Your ship shall sail.

But you must have known, seen it all, in the fire of your forge, burning on, in the long nights of your prairie dreams, for it was you that wrote these words: *Four times there will be men who will try to raise and assemble this ship. Three times they will fail, but a fourth man will succeed. He will start the raising of my ship and it will sail across the prairies at speeds unheard of in this day and age, and will disappear in a mighty roar. My ship will go up and I shall rest in peace.*

The hull: Forty-three feet in length, thirteen feet wide, and ten feet high.

You built the ribs first, with lapped oak planking. Tarred and chalked. Another layer of oak, over which you placed one-sixteenth of an inch sheet metal, the ends crimped and joined together.

The keel: Thirty feet long and nine feet high. Double-planked, tarred and chalked, and overlaid with sheets of galvanized iron laced together with unbroken lines of steel wire.

And who builds a ship like that?

On the prairie?

To do what?

Go where?

How?

Why?

And this man—.

Is insane.

A wheelhouse and sleeping quarters, eight feet high, varnished, with four-foot railings.

The boiler you built by the river, where you heated and rolled, five-eighths thick steel on a press you made yourself, that many today still marvel at and wonder how.

The fiddle you made pushing you on through the long nights of your prairie dreams.

Tom?

And there you are, a man alone, painting the ship of your dreams with the blood of your horse.

And you ate that horse.

All the instruments made by you: propeller, chains, pulleys, cylinders, bilge pump—a lifeboat too.

You look at the men putting their hands to their hats, their words in the cold drifting before you.

Your money is gone, and now you fix things for food, when the people can pay.

A man forged by his dreams scavenging for food, a wild prairie man, and you're ready to move it all to the river.

Seven years in the making.

You asked a neighbor to borrow their tractor.

No.

His neighbor too.

Another door shut on your face.

And yet another.

And this man—.

Is insane.

And so it was, just you and your horse and a handmade pole-winch, one rotation, twenty feet, and that's what you did, what it took.

Two years, two miles, and only fifteen miles to go.

My God, would you look at that hull. It must be what? Ten feet?

If it's a foot.

And the river draws what?

Eight feet.

More like six.

Such a waste.

All that money.

In the spring of '43 the drought ends, the river floods, and who's to say what a man can do?

They found your maps of chartered waters and calculations. Pages upon pages, for all the world to see. You'd float the sections on their sides, and assemble them later, next to deeper waters.

Tom?

You see the lights.

It's time to go.

Blue and red lights. Blue and red lights.

By the road.

It's getting dark.

The long road.

It's for your own good.

The Number Two road.

The snow breaks beneath your feet and you point. South. Six hundred miles.

And what I'd like to know, Tom, is can you hear your fiddle still, in these dreams now of your long prairie nights?

Tomi Jannus Alankola, "'Tom Sukanen," was born in Kurjenkya, Finland, September 23, 1878. He was institutionalized in North Battleford, Saskatchewan, 1939, where he died, April 23, 1943. His ship, the Sontianen, still stands today.

LIARS ON THE RUN

cowritten with Stella Del Mar

He wanted to put into words all the things they might be. If they could. And it began like that. In his mind, it began like that.

On the shore, rhythms receding. Forever. Once again. Words like sand, persistent, unobserved until shards formed fully blown beneath skin. Because Lou Reed died, because yours were blue and I'm tangled up in it.

Liars on the run.

When you said you couldn't leave, when human voices woke us and I . . . well, where else do drowned girls go?

Walking away with bloodied feet. I tried to write you out. Rethread the narrative with different lies, yet ours persist, this hurtling without headlights toward an impossible dawn.

One day. I want to.

In bodies or in words?

Both.

Bodies, body, my body, your body, and all these words again—words that are never not us again.

On the radio. Lou Reed.

We could run.

All these questions surfacing. And won't be submerged. Won't be sifted out. Only denied. But I won't—

Fall toward me? Lips touching. Just once.

Once and always.

And you'll tell me how it happened, where we fell between the spasm and desire, between our shadow selves tangled up in lies, these limbs, this impossible wanting.

Darkness catching us stumbling on bloodied feet along passages not followed, doors not opened, exits not taken, ending where?

A rose garden.

In the moonlight?

Because darkness isn't forever.

No. Or time.

Of time. Our time. This urgency of ghost light illuminating intuition. The movements of tides. You with me.

Here and breaking chains. Trying and smashing.

Spiraling?

Yes.

Urgency never receding. How does he mean that?

Next to me, and does it matter? Timeless and not moving, does it matter. All this fear and falling away, to your scent, this touch of you, seen and unseen, as it does, every time, in this garden. These lies in headlights, wild and not caring, are never lies, not really—running to me, and you say, where are you?

Tell it to me.

How?

In the mirror. Golden and not moving. Still, and always, and where are you?

In the falling of light—of course it is, over and over. Words that are us. Not us.

All this damage. And mine too.

Our flaws?

Yes. Together. Our flaws. How it could it not be?

Cresting a hill, harder and faster, and we'll outrun it all. I promise.

The road dropping. Ivy and open fields. And you say, show me. Real and here and show me.

In this wanting show me.

And I'll tell you, let's just take it all.

Baby, she wasn't just a part of me. I loved her too. Sometimes. And then I—take it all away and I find her gone. So young. Beautiful in her defaults.

Was she?

Reliving it next to me in a glory. So much of it that I didn't want to be gone. But it is now, isn't it?

Liars' lips and liars' lovers exorcising ghosts, no matter how many letters you burn, no matter what you sacrifice to the flames, then smudge away with sage.

I've seen the scars.

I look at you driving. Saying nothing more. Knowing you won't be denied. And I ask, can I outrun you?

No.

I've tried. Forgive me. Forgive me for wanting you when you go, and yet, here we are—reckless, still. And I can't run blind forever.

In the dark?

Hands clean, bloodied feet.

Not always. No.

You pull over to the side of the gravel road. And we move across a wide open space beneath an uncaring sky. A sky on which our choices scream from bodies of dying stars.

Walking. Fixed and fatal. And here we are again. Watching.

You're a dominant fire sign, and I want you—want you to try. Your warmth, your light. An undeniable truth before this reckoning, this coming of light only.

Is that what they say? Where is it? Show me. We stand and look.

Tall trees looming we must pass beneath in this urgency. Once again, together.

The ground wet, your hands tangle in my hair, you push me down. Capture my lips beneath yours, the hard truth of you above me, on me, grounding me and keeping me here.

These lies that sear. This pain I bring to you.

Eyes I see. Innocence crying needing.

Witness it, I whisper. Be part of it. In all the things we do, that we must leave here, under this dark unforgiving sky of better days ahead. Of once again—one day.

The trees above us, a witness now, as the wind to them. And I take it all from you, an unimaginable opening. My hand finding you, my other hand moving hair from your forehead, these streaks of what it must be, an opening made wider, cauterizing, there and more coming, trapped, held, your screaming—to the trees—to the birds, flying, in these days now that never will be again. My hands releasing you, and there's a scar, outside of you, long and hard and running: our always. Shall I tell you?

Yes. A single word hardly spoken, drifting from you by these things unseen, that we do, you and I, we witness. But not now, worlds away in our sleep. Finally. Worlds without ending, these forever worlds of infinite webs. Gossamer strands that bind. Wide open spaces falling through to darkness. A darkness well beyond any ghost light. Beyond dawn itself.

She looks for you, in the dark, pull her to you, down, down— far beneath this falling. And you whisper, in this rhythm, lie, baby, lie.

We walk again, and you ask me, how did we get here?

I'm looking around, in the cold hard morning light.

There was a car?

Yes.

We drove?

The last exit.

You take off your leather jacket and hand it to me. I'm alone.

No baby, I'm right here—the wind picking up, through the leaves, and now silent. In my arms silent. In this never not knowing: where we've been, where we are, where we're going.

Where you go.

Does it matter?

Kiss me.

Liars' lips and liars lie more, and once more.

This land us, barren and holding on—just, small scrubs and the growth of it. Trying. Rising. Broken missing pieces.

The one long road, empty and giving, somewhere. Is it?

We'll find our way back yet.

Will we?

Nothing in remorse in a line to anywhere, and you put your head to my shoulder and take my arm. Lou Reed on the radio somewhere.

Yes.

Let's just go.

Where?

Liars on the run.

In this place—.

No. Never again.

Liars' lips bodies in words again.

Always.

TWENTY OR THIRTY GRAND ON CHRISTMAS MORNING

W hat'ya doin?
I thought it might be 24-7.

What'ya need?

Smokes.

I got some. On the dash. Grab me one. He watches her. Jesus Christ, he thinks.

She lights a cigarette and passes him the lighter and the smokes. What'ya doin? With that chain, I mean, what'ya doin?

He stands and looks around, at the three a.m. darkness. I'm takin the cash machine.

The what?

The ATM. You know, the cash machine.

The whole machine?

Yup.

For the money?

Why else?

Why don't ya just smash it and take the money?

Ya can't, they ain't built like that. Otherwise, everyone would be walkin around smashin em, wouldn't they?

Aren't ya afraid you'll get caught?

Nope.

Why not? I would be. I don't think I could ever do somethin like that.

I've done it before.

You have.

Yup.

Lots of times?

Enough times.

How much money's in there?

Twenty or thirty grand. Sometimes more.

What if someone comes by?

You mean like you?

She doesn't answer and she toes out her cigarette. I won't say anything.

I know you won't.

They look at one another.

What's your name?

Daisy.

Daisy?

Yeah, Daisy Chainsaw.

Daisy Chainsaw, what a great name. I like it.

Thanks.

Wait, wasn't that a band?

Was, but they broke up, and it was available, so I took it.

Great band. All right, Daisy, time to step back, and he grabs a length of pipe from the back of the pickup and smashes out the door glass.

No alarm sounds and he knocks away the larger jagged pieces holding to the frame. He steps inside. Pass me the chain.

She does, and she stays bent over watching him wrap the chain around the cash machine.

That's it? That's all there is to it?

Yup, that's it, and he walks back out through the door opening. Smash and grab.

The American way.

Somethin like that. He sees a car. Fuck. He takes her arm. Kneel down.

They watch the car approaching, it's a cop, and he starts to unhook the chain from the truck.

She sees a gun tucked into the waist of his pants.

If they come this way, you can either run, or jump in with me, your choice.

The cruiser stops. White-blue tailpipe smoke, drifting in the cold early morning air.

He looks at Daisy. Well?

I should at least know your name?

Jay.

Really?

Yeah, why?

No reason. It's a nice name. What about the money?

What about it?

You're just gonna leave it?

There's other money.

There is?

Yup.

On Christmas morning?

Nope, not this Christmas morning, I guess. But there's no shortage of cash machines, and other days, that's for damn sure.

No, I guess that's right.

Merry Christmas, Daisy.

Yeah, Merry Christmas to you too, Jay.

And that's it, the snow starts to fall and the cop drives on, and they've got twenty or thirty grand on Christmas morning.

RIDING A BIKE THROUGH THE LONELY CONTINUUM OF TIME

His name was Leonard. He was riding a bike. His arms held out to the sides of him, his mind never trapped by his own self, never buckling under the weight of what he should be, or shouldn't be, understanding the truth of himself, always, in this world, hard as that was, and of course, in this moment too, riding a bike through the lonely continuum of time. He smiled at his knowing, where others couldn't—or fucking wouldn't, and he was right, and knew he was right, and always would be.

He rode on, his arms still there, to the sides of him, and he said, come, cover me. Gliding and dipping and soaring, and we do, going on and on, down a lonely, long road, and free now, or at least so he thought. Free and wanting.

Free and needing.

And who among us would not say, such a person as this.

He turned and smiled, reaching his hands up to the breaking blue sky, and he said, yes yes yes, I am here now.

On either side of the road started to appear large outcroppings of shield rock streaked with black and pink and where alder bushes, raspberry bushes, and trees grew from crevices.

He saw ancient trees grown too tall and heavy for their rocky moorings, having fallen onto their sides, great circular walls of exposed roots and dirt pointing to the sky.

He rode past dark and vacant lakes, and he rode past narrow long stretches of washed-out lowlands, sun-bleached trees still standing, dead and broken.

He was tired, and walking the bike now, the sun not yet down, the moon there, and he looked up to it, and said, love under a big moon.

Why wouldn't there be?

Of course there would be.

Probably was and just forgotten.

Probably was.

He stopped and looked around, and he thought, what else might be out there?

Endless possibilities of strange and wonderful things.

He looked back up to that everyone's one big moon. Ain't that right, moon?

Ain't it now, said the moon back to him.

Why I'm here.

Always will be.

True enough, and always will be.

And he was happy, walking, a coyote following him high up on the granite ridgeline, stopping, looking too, at that everyone's one big moon.

On a night such as this.

He came upon a house set back from the road. He dropped the bike and walked up the long gravel driveway.

The house was white stucco, cracked and chipped and stained with dirt. Tall weeds running up the walls.

To the right of the house, a clapboard garage the same color as the house.

He looked for a dog, or any sign of a dog. There wasn't one. Not that he could tell.

He walked to the garage and stopped and looked back at the house. He reached for the garage door handle and pulled, the door lifting up from the ground toward him, a stack of aluminum folding chairs tipping over. He paused, holding the door handle, two weighted cylinders filled with rocks, one on either side of the door, swaying from thin strands of twisted wire.

A second-story light came on and he let go of the handle to see if the door would stay. It did, and he moved toward the back of the house.

The back light came on, mosquitoes swarming the brightness. An old man wearing pajamas and a frayed striped bathrobe appeared. His grey hair disheveled. His watery, hooded eyes, squinting. A single-barrel shotgun in his hand. Who's there?

He pushed open the screen door to the hum of the evening heat and the sound of the mosquitoes bouncing off the glass of the small light. Well?

He stepped onto the porch boards, the screen door slapping shut behind him. I won't ask again.

He walked forward and Leonard stepped out from behind the house, wrapping his left arm around the man's neck. Shh, he said.

The old man eye's widening. He didn't struggle.

Leonard pressed the cold tip of a clip-blade knife to the man's throat. It's me.

The old man. Who?

The one ya been waitin for, and he ran the knife through the thin, slack skin of the old man's neck.

He looked at the blood, pooling on the broken patio stones. He looked at the closed screen door and the light behind the door.

An old woman called from the house. Horace?

He looked to the second-story window.

Is everything all right?

He stepped over the man bleeding out beneath him and he entered the house.

The old woman appeared at the window, the soft bedroom light behind her highlighting the frailness of her thin frame beneath her long white nightgown. Horace?

Leonard appeared in the window, approaching the woman from behind, the old woman turning, and screaming.

He woke and sat up in the old couple's bed and looked at the woman beneath the window on the floor, her nightgown soaked in blood, a long stream of it having run from her. He turned on the bed and placed his boots on the well waxed hardwood floor and he lowered his head and closed his eyes and ruffled his hair. He looked up at an antique vanity desk across from the bed.

He sat on the chair and opened a jewelry box and ran his fingers through it, an old broach, a charm bracelet, several pairs of earrings, a pearl necklace and matching pearl earrings. He fisted it all and put it in his coat pocket. He looked back at the old woman and stood and walked to her.

He squatted and took her left hand into his, sizing up her diamond ring and wedding band. He tried to pull them off. They wouldn't come. He pulled harder. He took his knife out and opened the blade. He folded back the other fingers of her hand and pressed her hand to the floor and pushed the blade through the crunch of bone. He slid the rings off the backside of her freed finger and dropped the finger to the floor. He cleaned the blade on her nightgown and folded the knife closed. He tilted his head, looking at the old woman's opened eyes, and he wondered, what was in there still?

Anything?

Doubt it.

Would it make a difference?

Probably not.

I bet they're thankin ya?

Bet they are too.

If they could.

Why wouldn't they?

She seemed like someone's nice old grandma.

He stood and pocketed the rings, and he walked down the stairs.

Like they'd lived here a long time.

I guess.

And they might of been happy.

I didn't put em in my path, someone else done that. And if there's a reason for that, there's a reason for me.

No doubt. Everything else is just made up, ain't it?

True enough, just made up. Heaven or hell. Except I ain't, and I never will be.

He lifted the kettle from the stove and poured out the water and refilled it. He placed it back on the stove, turned the element on, and looked in the fridge. He closed it and walked out the back door.

He stepped back over the dead old man and the patio stone blood and walked toward the garage. He lifted the garage door and looked at the cluttered mess. There wasn't even a car. Nothing much there at all.

He walked back to the house and up the stairs and walked inside.

He lifted the whistling kettle from the stove and searched through the cupboards until he found a jar of instant coffee. He made a strong mug of black coffee and carried it to the table. He sat and crossed his legs and took a sip. He lit a cigarette, and he smoked, and he drank his coffee.

On a night such as this.

Love under a big moon

That's what he thought.

QUITTING SMOKING

Interior: A tin drive-shed.

I wish ya could sew my mouth up.

Jake and Jared, two brothers, drinking beer, sitting on blocks of dried cracked white oak.

Funny, said Jared, I do too.

A grease-stained fridge and a grease-stained concrete pad. A garbage can surrounded by empty auto parts boxes, dirty rags, discarded bottles and cans, and assorted other trash.

I'm serious. I gotta quit these fuckin things. They're killin me.

How would ya eat?

That's a good question.

You could use a straw.

Wouldn't work. If I could put a straw in there, I could put a smoke in there.

What if we sewed it in there good and tight?

A long workbench down the one side, an unused hoist in the center of the room. Posters of girls and cars. A bottle of whiskey and empty beer cans.

Would ya do it?

What? Sew your mouth up?

Yeah.

Sure I would, I guess, but it'll hurt like hell.

We got this whiskey, and I ain't feelin too much pain already. Ya got a needle? Maybe one of them big hook ones they use, make it easier?

I doubt it.

Any thread?

Thread wouldn't work, you could snap it too easy just opening your mouth. Needs to be stronger.

Where's your fishing gear?

Right over there.

Well?

Well what?

We could use that.

That's a damn good idea. Let me get it.

Take your time.

What 'bout this?

What 'bout one of them bigger bait-hook ones?

This one?

Yeah.

What pound line? Six or eight?

Better make it eight, I get powerful urges.

Let me thread it up. How's the whiskey?

Goin down smooth. Hey?

What?

When was the last time you used that hook?

I don't know, let me think. I caught that big bass on it, remember that?

Helluva fish.

Was.

I'm thinking though—

What's that?

Maybe we'd better sterilize it.

Probably should. Pass the lighter.

Here ya go.

How's this?

A little more.

Ya think this is enough line?

Should be. What about the straw?

I dunno if we got one. I'll have a look.

He fires up a smoke. Take your time.

Found one.

Great.

Ya ready.

Nope. Let me finish this last smoke.

I seen they had a boot drive on the bridge this morning.

Yup, I saw it too. He takes another sip. I got stuck in it.

Ya give anythin?

I only had some change on me, but I had a couple of new boxes of shells and I gave em one of those.

That was good of ya.

I thought so. Horrible thing, all them poor kids.

Fuckin crazy bastard. I'd like to put a hole in em.

Hashtag me too.

What?

Ready? He butts his smoke out. Wait.

What?

Gimme the straw.

Yeah, right, here ya go.

How's that?

More to the center.

Good?

Yup. Better grip that chair, I don't want ya punching me.

I ain't gonna punch ya, just get it done.

All right, but damn this is gonna hurt. Hold still.

Shit!

You dropped the damn straw.

Sorry, but that hurt like a mother.

Take another drink.

Ya, I'd better.

Ready?

Hold on, the straw. How's this?

Good.

I won't say a thing this time, I promise.

Ya better not, and stay still.

There we go. That's a fine job if I don't say so myself. Here, let me get a rag, ya got a lot of blood comin out of there.

That's better. Try and open your mouth.

Good, ya can't do it. Does it hurt?

What? You wanna drink? Hold on.

Here ya go, suck some up.

Look at that, works great.

What'ya doin now?

Why ya reaching for your smokes? Ya can't smoke, we sewed your mouth up.

Would ya look at that? We didn't think about that. Did it just come to ya now?

What was the point of sewing your mouth up? Smoking through the straw like that? We need a smaller straw, so your smoke won't fit in the end of it.

Ya look damn stupid, I'll can tell ya that.

Evening, boys—what the hell?

Oh, hey, Sugar.

My god, what have ya done?

What?

What the hell have ya done to Jake?

Nothing. He wanted to quit smokin.

Well, it don't seem to be workin so good, does it? He's smoking one now.

I know he is. We need a smaller straw. Think we got one?

I don't know, I'll have a look.

CASH, GUNS, BOOZE AND WHORES: DESPERATION NEVER WINS

I t was a failed attempt.
We needed to keep going.

I'm a boy peddling a bike hard down a gravel road toward a distant world of my own making.

And see me now, at the world's largest airport terminal—arrested.

South Korea.

Did you know there were entire worlds beneath these conduits to other places? Detention centers, interrogation rooms, law-enforcement offices, a prosecutor's office, a court room and judge—and boom, just like that, from jail to guilty and on an Interpol list.

I had been caught leaving the country with twenty grand in cash. Yeah, I know—a mistake I wouldn't normally make, but the night before had been a late one, and I had been rushing to make my flight.

What's four grand among friends, pay the fine and move on.

Problem was, I was on my way to Russia, and I still had sixteen grand, six more than I was legally allowed to travel with, and now, having missed my flight, I had to loop through Hong Kong—two more international lines to cross.

I could either find someone in line and ask them if they'd mind holding six grand for me as we cleared customs, or I could start stuffing cash in all my things.

I surveyed the other passengers on the plane—who?

She seemed nice, but not too nice, and we started chatting. I explained I had come into twenty grand while in Korea, and the problems I was having travelling with it, and would she mind holding six of it while we cleared customs?

For twenty percent?

WTF? I was starting to feel like Hemingway's fish.

Fifteen.

Twenty.

Fine.

Cash, guns, booze, and whores.

Russia.

Black Land Rovers and E-Series BMWs, drivers with guns, and beautiful girls.

I'd met up with the others, a former World's Strongest Man— a hard-ass, when he wanted to be, and a giant Scottish man, tipping the scales at well over four hundred pounds, a PhD in geology, and drinking, and world class at that, no matter where we were, Asia, South America, Iceland, the Baltic states, the Eastern Bloc, and of course, Russia. He could put away twenty or thirty ounces of vodka and a half dozen beers—have a safe night boys, and off he'd go to bed. And only one time did I see him miss the elevator and walk into the wall. He was a good friend, and I miss him still.

Lunch in a Japanese restaurant—and now we're not, we're in a backroom behind a steel door without handles. And there he was, with two women, his arm around the one, talking to me through his representative, "Natasha." And behind him? Let's just call him—well, you didn't call him anything. He seemed all right, for what he was, which was what? Never far from the man.

That night.

In a nightclub owned by him, like so many other things, other clubs, restaurants, magazines, and every billboard in Moscow. A Putin trickle-down friend, or so we'd come to learn later. The next time I saw him, I was in Columbus, Ohio. He thought he'd come and take in an event. He was greeted by the FBI and detained for seventy-two hours, just because they could, just to let him know they knew who he was and that he was there.

Later.

Three in the morning later—and you want to do what? Pile in the cars with the drivers, the guns, the beautiful girls, and head out of the city to the woods and drink vodka and shoot deer?

What'd I do?

I drank the vodka, popped a few rounds, and thought of Hunter.

Sunday Morning.

Red Square and it hit home. I was feeling a little under the weather and lagging behind Natasha and the hard-ass from steel-town UK. I rounded a corner and was swarmed by a pack of street kids holding up fur hats for sale and looking to pickpocket me. Natasha turned around and yelled his name and that was it, they scattered. That's when I knew, steel-town too, we looked at one another, and we could tell we were saying the same thing to ourselves at the same time: fuck.

Being Sunday, Lenin's tomb was closed. It didn't matter. Natasha talked to the guard and that was it, in we went.

All-in-all, none of this turned out so well. Surprising? It shouldn't have been, but there was no, all is not right in Oz. No, Dorothy get me home.

Desperation never wins.

RAISE YOUR VOICE UP

What do you want me to say? You're breaking my heart? Fine.

But what's that to you? Wrap yourself in it and repair yourself. Tough as hell and big fucking deal, because at the end of all of this, where's that? Nowhere. Alone and coming fast—too fast, this home of ours and nowhere here now.

Good for you, and don't bring me all the things that might have been. I'm not interested. Bring me everything else. Bring me you.

Or you can't?

Where's your courage? Your voice? Gone. Gutter gone and ain't coming back, I guess.

Put your phone down and raise your voice up—for only, if we the people—

Too far down the sloping shoulders of this world, of this particular dark hole, this day. Keep your yesterdays of what was. What wasn't.

Was sure it could be. One day.

Alone and holding on, and don't be sad.

Where's the light of this enlightenment you said we could be? Don't bury it with you. But you do.

They're not you and they're not me and they never will be and boys will be boys and all of that but I ain't and neither are you. Better than all of that.

Better than all of that always.

Were we?

Show me.

And so you look around and ask yourself, where's this pain? I won't play that game. But you might think otherwise.

Just like George Floyd.

And so don't.

Break my heart.

Go.

Go now.

Burn it.

Burn it now and burn it all down.

THE LIGHTHOUSE, THE PIER, AND THE WOMAN

In the year of her darkness, there were no sounds of summer, no turning of leaves in the crisp autumn air. Only the despair in the long nights of her winter.

That day.

Calm and quiet, the cold wind of an early spring fresh upon their young pale cheeks, red now, and they smiled.

From the northeast, a sudden storm, the cool calm waters raging.

Unnavigable waters.

She told the world: I'll let you know if I need you, and she locked the doors, shut the windows, and drew the curtains.

Every Saturday morning she retrieved her grocery and liquor store deliveries from the porch, occasionally looking up and seeing her neighbors, walking, standing, talking on street corners. She'd close the door on their vicious looks and rumors—this world that was not hers now, and never would be again.

She spent the morning of the one year anniversary of their deaths in bed, restless, drinking cups of coffee, looking at magazines and books.

She took her pills and stared at the closed curtains. Her mind blank, the way she'd trained it to be. Only the darkness. Until she was gone. Released again. Just not always.

She woke and poured a glass of red wine and paced the empty house.

At the children's closed bedroom door, her hand to the paneled wood.

Their voices.

That scent.

The touch of them.

Crumpled on the floor, for how long? She didn't know.

She walked to her room and sat on the bed and she told herself, you can do it.

She pulled the covers over her, curled up, and slept again.

She woke and drank a glass of wine while looking for something to wear. A pair of jeans and a heavy hand-knit sweater.

She poured another glass of wine and walked down the stairs. She laced her boots and put on her husband's old, tan, canvas coat that sadly no longer smelt of him.

She finished her wine and placed the empty glass on the narrow hallway table. She looked at the lamp. At its heavy glass base. She removed the shade, pulled the cord, picked it up and opened the door and stepped outside.

The dampness in the air felt good; it was cold and fresh on her face. The heaviness of the lamp felt good, reassuring. She walked the quiet empty streets, old houses hidden behind old trees, keepers of strange and secret things.

At the top of a hill above the harbor, she stopped and looked at the open sea.

Rolling whitecaps.

A slight wind pushing in from the northeast.

She walked the long concrete pier, waves breaking over large rocks lining the pier, her eyes fixed upon the water, not noticing the light rain that had begun to fall.

She stopped next to an old lighthouse, worn and rusted from too many years of neglect and stormy weather. Its stories of past worlds remaining untold.

The wind picking up.

The rain coming harder.

A wave breaking over the end of the pier, raining down upon her.

With each new wave, she remained, unmoving.

The sky darkening.

Larger waves yet approaching.

Lightning.

She stepped closer to the edge of the pier, waiting.

A wave exploding, knocking her back, and sucking her from the pier.

In the cold water, turning, her eyes wide open, the lamp cord wrapping around her.

Sinking—falling. Once again.

She closed her eyes, and she reached her hand out to the paneled wood.

The old lighthouse in the storm. Another tale untold, taken to its rusty grave.

THE WITCH IN THE WOODS

Development had come, it always does, eventually. Old trees taken down and new ones planted. Big new houses with only slight variations between them. Doors and trim painted in bright individualized colors.

Friendships made, groups and clubs, kids playing.

It wasn't all gone, of course, all the yesterdays, a certain type of living. Across the road, at the edge of this new subdivision, was a forest, thick with old trees, bushes overgrown, the grass wild with weeds, and places too, where it would not grow. And set far back in this forest was an old house.

An intimidating place, full of mystery and wonder, especially if you were a young girl or boy growing up across the road on the quiet, safe streets of a new subdivision. A place where the main topics of discussion always seemed to be, who was having a barbeque? Who was having trouble at work? New cars. Who was having an affair with who?

But then, of course, there was that house.

Set far back from the road in the woods like that.

Why wouldn't they sell?

Hidden away and rundown.

Who lived there?

Why would they want to?

A mad, crazy woman.

A witch, of course.

What else?

Alice was with all the other children. She was tiny, one of the smallest ones, with a face full of freckles. She was mighty, at least that's what she told all the other kids, and her older brother, Edward, of course too. He'd just laugh, and she'd have to punch him.

It was a rite of passage to be the one, and she was determined to be that one.

They'd been there now for over an hour, after their dinners, all of them saying they'd be the one. And yet, no one had moved. They hadn't dared to.

"Let's do it together?"

Each one waiting for the other one to start, and it was almost dark now. And who would do it then?

Alice stood. "I'll go."

No one moved.

"You Alice?" said her brother, Edward, and he began to laugh.

The others laughed too.

"Why not? I'm not afraid."

"She'll eat you alive," said one of the other boys.

"You're no bigger than a button," said one.

"She might turn ya into something," said Edward's best friend, Andy. "A toad maybe."

"Or stake you up in the cellar," said another boy. "And save you for later."

Alice put her hands to her hips and looked at each one of them. "You just wait and see if I don't. Stay here. Don't leave. I'll be right back."

The other kids fell silent, looking at one another, not believing their ears.

"You're not really going to do it," asked Edward. "Are you, Alice?"

She looked at her brother. "Of course I am. I'm not afraid." And oh God, she thought, please don't let them see me shake, for in fact, she was frightened to death. But she knew, there was no turning back now.

"Don't forget about them bushes," said one of the boys.

"That's right, Alice. Don't forget about them bushes," said Andy. "She'll have ya for sure then, cold with your blood still warm."

"Think that's real?" asked Alice.

"Of course it is," said Andy.

"Everyone knows it is," said another boy.

"There's only one spot in and out that's safe," said Edward. "All the other thorns are tipped with poison. Everyone knows it. Just wait and see, all the bones of dead squirrels and things like that."

"We could do it tomorrow," said Alice's best friend, Liv, the only other girl in the group. "I'd come with ya then."

"Nope, I'm doing it now," said Alice. "It's now or never. I'm goin and that's it, and I'm not afraid."

"Don't forget to bring back a little silver bell, or it won't count," said one of the boys.

"Jimmy," said Alice, "where'd your brother say it was safe to pass through? Tell me again."

The only one in the history of the development to have made it back with a little silver bell. Jimmy's older brother, Tommy.

"To the left of the old walkway. That's what he said. Said he got lucky."

"Here, Alice," said Liv, "wear my coat. It might protect ya while crawling under them poisonous bushes."

"Thanks," said Alice, and she put the coat on and started on her way. She looked back. "Don't leave without me. Wait for me."

"We'll be right here," said Liv.

"Promise?"

"Yes, promise," said Liv. "Of course we will. Be careful. I love you."

"I love you too. But don't worry, I'll be back."

"If we hear ya screamin," said Edward, "we'll run and get help."

"Thanks," said Alice. "But don't tell Mom and Dad whatever you do." And she turned back around and started walking.

She worked her way through the woods slowly, stopping, listening.

An owl called.

She looked up, and she wished the moon was bigger, and brighter, the day less cloudy.

She made her way to a big oak tree and stopped, peeking out at the house. There were lights on in the house, and a porch light on.

She waited a little longer, and not seeing anyone moving in the house, she stepped out from behind the tree and walked crouched over toward the house, being careful not to step on any dead tree branches or crunchy leaves. She made it to the bushes and crouched down farther. There were no sounds and she couldn't see anyone in the house, and then—oh my God, there they were, a long string of little silver bells, strung end-to-end across the porch. Just like Jimmy's brother had said.

She looked and saw the old stone pathway, mostly covered with moss and dead leaves. She didn't see any dead squirrel bones, or dead cats, nothing like that. Maybe they'd all been recently cleared away? She looked at the bushes to the left of the path, spotting an area just high enough for her to fit under. It'd be tight, but she thought she could make it.

She stretched out on her belly, pressing herself to the earth, and turned her head. She closed her eyes and exhaled the air out of herself and started to crawl forward. She stopped, trying to press herself tighter to the ground. She started to move again when she heard the screen door open. Oh my God no, she thought. I'm a goner. She'll have me for sure. Please please please, don't eat me.

She heard an old woman's voice. "What are you doing on your belly like some poor fool? Stand up."

She didn't know what to do. She was too scared to move, and she didn't want to open her eyes. Don't cry, she thought, and don't start to shake. She had to let out the air she was holding in her lungs.

"Go on, get up. I won't boil and eat you, I promise. I've already had my supper."

She opened her eyes and looked up at the old witch. She looked away quickly, just in case she might turn to stone.

"Well? Get off the ground like some poor sick creature. Find your backbone, and just do it."

She pushed herself backward, slowly, out from under the bushes. She started to stand, thinking, maybe she should run? And she did.

"Stop!"

She froze.

"You've a thorn caught on your coat, you might rip it." The old woman pointed. "See it there. Unhook it."

Alice looked again at the witch. She seemed ancient, small and frail and slightly bent forward. Grey hair in a bun at the back of her head. Otherwise, her clothes seemed kind of old person normal, no black dress or black cape or pointy hat, nothing like that, just a summer dress with a pretty cardigan and black leather shoes with wide stubby heels.

She looked at her friend's coat. She didn't want to touch the branch with the poisonous thorns.

"They're not poisonous, for goodness sake. It's just a rose bush."

She looked again at the thorn hooked into the coat. She reached for the branch, being careful not to touch the thorns.

And she thought, should she still run? Before it was too late? She wanted to, but she looked at the silver bells, and she knew if she did, she wouldn't have one of those to show the others.

"Is that what you've come for? One of my little silver bells?"

Alice nodded.

"You're the brave one amongst your group, I see. Come up here."

Alice didn't move.

"If you want one of my little silver bells, you're going to have to trust me. The pathway is just a little overgrown, that's all. Push the branch forward, like a gate, and come up here."

She looked back toward the road.

"If you're too frightened of a silly old rose bush, then go ahead and run away. But you won't get one of those." And she pointed to the string of silver bells hanging from the porch ceiling.

Alice tucked her hand into the sleeve of her coat and pushed the branch forward, like a gate, and she stepped through the open space.

"There now, look at that, you did it. Well done, and you're still breathing, I see. C'mon up here and have a seat."

She walked up the porch stairs, looking above her at the string of silver bells.

"What's your name?"

"Alice."

"Have a seat, Alice, and we'll have ourselves a proper little chat, like decent neighbors do. Would you like a glass of lemonade?"

With antifreeze, Alice thought. She heard herself saying, "Yes, please."

"Sit there and I'll be right back."

How was she gonna explain this? And what about Jimmy's brother? Those bushes weren't poisonous at all. And as far as she could tell, she wasn't even a witch. In fact, she seemed kind of nice and somewhat normal, for an old person living alone in the woods. "That lying—"

"Pardon me?"

"Oh, I'm sorry, ma'am."

"I should hope so. Here we go." She handed Alice a glass of lemonade and sat in the chair next to her. "It's good to see I'm still that old witch with poisonous bushes that killed her sister. I'd hate to think I'd lost my touch."

Alice looked at the woman. "You know about that?"

"Of course I do. I've known about it for a long time. There were houses there before all of your new ones, you know. Not as many, of course, but enough, and there have always been young boys and girls telling tall tales and seeking adventure, at least, for as long as I can remember."

"You mean, it's not true?"

"It's Alice, right?"

"Yes."

"What's a witch, Alice? An old woman who lives on her own? Is that all it takes? No special powers? No flying brooms? If that's the case, the world is filled with witches. God willing, you'll be old yourself one day, and what will that make you? A witch too? My sister was a dear sweet woman whom I loved very much. And I miss her to this day." She looked at the string of silver bells. "That's

why I have those. I put one out each year on the anniversary of her death. Thirty-five, so far. And do you know why?"

Alice shook her head.

"Because, when the wind blows, they chime, and it makes me think it's her, come back home for a visit. And that comforts me. It comforts me a great deal."

Alice looked again at the string of silver bells.

"Would you like one?"

She looked at the woman and nodded.

"Well, then, we'll have to come to an understanding."

"An understanding?"

"Yes, you may have one of my little silver bells, to take back and show your friends, as your badge of courage—which, by the way, you were, very brave, and not only that, the first girl ever to make it here, and I'm so very proud of you for that. Yes, indeed, I am. It certainly took long enough. However, in exchange for one of my little silver bells, you will have to promise me, you'll continue with the myth of the witch in the woods."

"I will? Why?"

"You most certainly will. And why? Because it, too, has become a comfort to me. A mask I have come to enjoy wearing. Besides, I really don't want to be bothered by an endless stream of good-willed, or otherwise, people. And I look at it this way, I get to meet only the bravest of the brave. Not knowing when the next young one, like yourself, will show up, and it's always a welcome surprise. And then we have a visit, like you and I are now, and on their way they go. Until they come back, unknown to the others, and we have longer visits, getting to know one another better. Watching them grow, their lives unfolding before me. And I have come to enjoy this very much."

"They come back?"

"Yes, of course they do. Not all, but most of them do."

"Did Jimmy's brother come back?"

"Do you mean, Tommy? The tall skinny one that was here a few years ago?"

"Yes, Tommy Johnson."

"No. But perhaps he will yet."

"Can I come back?"

"Yes, of course you can, I would like that very much, and as often as you like. But remember, you only just escaped with your life, having snuck under my poisonous bushes, evading my evil powers, with your little silver bell clutched tightly in your hand." She held out her closed hand. "Go on, hold your hand out."

Alice held her hand out and the woman placed a little silver bell there.

She looked at the bell. She couldn't believe it. Wait until the others see this.

"Go on then, you mustn't keep your friends waiting."

"Thank you."

"You're welcome, Alice. And don't forget our arrangement. You promise?"

"Yes, I promise. I won't forget."

"One more thing. When you look at that bell, do not only think of me, but of your bravery, and how in facing your fears, something good came of it—a lasting friendship."

"Thank you, I will." And Alice walked down the stairs, stopping at the rose bush.

"Like a gate."

She looked back at the old woman making the motion of pulling back a gate.

Alice reached for the branch and took hold of it between the thorns and pulled it back toward her, slipping through the opening. She turned and looked back at the woman. "Goodbye, and thank you. I'll be back for a visit. I promise!"

"I know you will." And the old woman watched Alice running through the woods, beneath the light of the moon, a little silver bell clutched tightly in her hand.

And just like that, the old woman snapped her fingers, and she was gone.

ON MY WAY TO SUNDAY

Most days, sometimes several times a day, Elizabeth would ask herself, where's my life in all of this? Arenas and music recitals, dentist appointments, work, dinners, cleaning up—worn down and aging. Too fast. When nothing is great, it's all good, and what could be worse than that?

And her husband?

Did he notice?

Did he care?

When really, she was still young and attractive, at least, that's what she thought. And yet, spin class wasn't cutting it anymore.

She got out of her SUV and closed the door. Her heels on the damp pavement, clipping in the early morning mist.

Her morning place. Coffee, pastry, and a long line.

There was an older couple in front of her. They seemed nice. Chatty. Friendly to one another. As if they still cared.

It was always busy this time on a weekday.

She looked behind her, and their eyes met. That woman.

Morning.

Elizabeth heard herself say, morning, and she turned away, her face flushed. Why? She had no idea. It was weird, and it had begun to frustrate her.

The line moved.

She felt awkward, and she hated that too. Don't look back.

A nonfat chai tea latte, please.

It had been going on for some time, and frankly, puzzlement and wonderment were not her specialties.

The woman ordered a tall Americano. She looked at Elizabeth, waiting for her nonfat chai tea latte, and she took a pen from her pocket and picked up a napkin from the counter and put them in front of Elizabeth. Write your number down. We'll get a drink sometime.

Elizabeth looked at the pen and napkin in front of her, and she looked at the woman. She wrote her number down and slid the napkin back to her.

And that was it, the woman, Rebecca, picked up her coffee and the napkin and left.

Elizabeth took hers and left.

And who saw that coming?

Random and a little weird.

Perhaps they'll become friends?

Elizabeth might like that, someone outside of her usual set of friends, a little more interesting. Artistic, perhaps? Certainly, somewhat different.

And she wondered, should she feel worried?

Concerned?

She didn't, in fact, she felt happy. Or rather, at least, not unhappy. A little nervous and not unhappy. And she didn't know why.

Driving her son home from his practice that night, her phone rang. A number not in her contacts.

Her son looked at her. Are you going to get it?

She answered the call, putting the phone to her ear.

Are you kidding me?

She gave her son a look.

Hello?

Elizabeth?

Yes.

It's Rebecca. How are you for tomorrow night? Eight o'clock at the same place?

Eight o'clock? Yes, that's fine.

Great, I'll see you then.

Who was that?

Someone from work.

The phone rang. It was her husband. She put it on Bluetooth.

Hey.

Hi.

Can you get Grace?

What?

I'm running a little late.

I'm on my way home with Robbie?

Sorry.

I think we can make it.

Great, thanks. And there he was, with several other men, all in suits and overcoats, entering a brown brick building with heavy black wooden doors. He held back. See you tonight, and thanks again. He hung up and entered the building. The sign above the door, The Brass Rail.

In a warm tub, kids settled, she wondered again, why? Why it happened? Why she let it happen? Why she agreed to meet?

Her husband was stretched out on the bed, his laptop open.

With a towel wrapped around her, another one around her hair, she began to look through her closet.

Jeans for sure.

What top?

I'm out tomorrow night.

Boots?

Oh?

She looked back. He was still on his laptop, pages of work spread out on the bed.

I might be late.

All right.

You'll need to pick up something for you and the kids to eat.

She waited, and he didn't answer.

She was early, in the car waiting, and she thought, she looked good, felt good.

She didn't have to go. She could just leave.

But would she?

Validation.

Who doesn't want to be seen and noticed and accounted for?

She checked her lipstick.

Fuck it, and she checked the time. One minute to eight.

She left the car and walked toward the coffee shop. She reached the door and opened it. Before she stepped inside, she paused, looking back at us, and together we think, this not *The Winter of Our Discontent*, this is next generation.

She entered and looked around the coffee shop, but couldn't see her.

Elizabeth?

She turned and saw Rebecca seated at a table next to the door.

You look lovely. Have a seat. A nonfat chai tea latte, right?

Yes, thank you. She sat. Her coat still on, and she reached for her drink.

Nervous?

Not really. More . . . curious, I would say.

Yes, I understand.

Why you asked to meet?

Rebecca sipped her coffee. We've seen each other here now for how long?

I'm not sure?

Six or seven months? Perhaps longer?

Yes, at least that.

Why shouldn't we get to know one another? What is this world otherwise? Although, it is true, one must be careful. But only to a degree.

Yes, true.

You don't know who I am, do you?

You? No.

Jelinek.

That Jelinek?

Yes.

Oh.

And what is it you do?

Real estate.

That can be rewarding.

It can also be a lot of work.

I imagine it can be. Kids?

Two. Robbie's fifteen, Grace thirteen. You?

No.

Married?

No. C'mon, leave your tea.

Sorry?

I want to show you something.

They left the coffee shop and Rebecca took a helmet from her parked matte black Triumph Street Twin and passed it to Elizabeth.

This is yours?

Yes. Rebecca put her helmet on and got on the bike and started it up. She looked back at Elizabeth. Ready?

Elizabeth nodded and got on the bike, wrapping her arms around Rebecca.

They moved through the quiet downtown, a few people walking, the sun low and setting behind them. They continued east, and soon there were rows of houses. Elizabeth began to relax, trusting more, leaning into Rebecca. Becoming aware of this, Rebecca opened up the bike.

The hum of the bike fell away and it was all just motion now, and it felt good. It felt free. The rows of houses stopping, narrow sections of woods to the south, rolling green hills with trees to the north, a brick wall and a black wrought iron fence atop of it, running for miles next to them.

Rebecca slowed the bike, running down the gears, and at a wide entrance to a paved driveway she pulled in and stopped in front of a tall black wrought iron gate. There was an unattended gatehouse. A camera mounted on the corner of the roof.

Rebecca punched in the code on the keypad and the gate began to open. She dropped the bike into gear and drove up the driveway.

More rolling green hills with perfectly manufactured gardens cut into the faces of the hills that lined the driveway.

Tall old oak trees.

The paved driveway, still coming.

To their left, an old mansion with ivy-covered red brick and a massive blue-grey slate roof. Half a dozen brick chimneys. A long tall row of trimmed cedar hedges. Rows of low trimmed boxwoods encasing colorful gardens. A large fountain out front.

Farther up the driveway, to the right, another house, red brick and old, too, but not as large. Out front of it, more well attended, manicured gardens.

Beyond a stand of tall ash trees, Elizabeth could see a racetrack for horses, lined with a black post-and-rail fence, a long low stable with a black tin roof, a steeple and spire at the front.

The driveway split around an island of birch trees centered by a tall sculpture of some sort. Rebecca took the bike right, leaning into the turn, and coming to a stop in front of a large board and baton grey building. There were gardens here as well and large glass lanterns on either side of large dark-stained doors.

They got off the bike and removed their helmets, Rebecca taking Elizabeth's from her. She put the helmets on the bike seat and walked to the doors and unlocked and opened them. She looked back at Elizabeth. Coming?

Rebecca turned the lights on. It was one massive room, a studio.

Elizabeth entered, looking around. She looked at Rebecca. This is incredible.

A large chandelier hung from the center of the ceiling over a large work-space counter. A sitting area was to their right, with several chairs and couches, a television mounted over a stone-and-glass fireplace. A bar with a kitchen area. There were paintings on the walls, and more of them stacked in rows to the back right. To their left, a large work-in-progress iron sculpture, at least twelve feet in height. There was a portable staircase pushed up to it. It was of a mother, leaning back, twirling her young daughter by her hands, the girl's hair flying back behind her, her dress ruffling. To the back left, other sculptures. Some finished, others not, all different shapes and sizes, and done in different mediums.

You're an artist?

Yes. Rebecca took her coat off and hung it on a coat rack by the door. She came back to get Elizabeth's but found her walking toward the large sculpture. Hearing Rebecca approaching, Elizabeth looked back. This is amazing. It truly is.

Thank you. Let me take your coat. I'll get us a drink.

She took Elizabeth's coat and hung it up and walked to the bar. She opened a bottle of red wine and poured two glasses. She walked back to Elizabeth and handed one to her. I'll show you around?

Yes, please. I'd like that.

Rebecca walked her through her collection of paintings, mostly mixed media collages. Some minimalist landscapes and figures.

You're very talented.

Thank you.

I love them all. You have such a distinctive style. They're incredible, really.

Rebecca moved behind the counter, looking at a work-in-progress design of some sort. She looked up at Elizabeth. Do you enjoy real estate?

Most of the time. There's parts of it I could live without. She watched Rebecca, bent over her work, her glass of wine in her hand, her hair falling to one side, down to the table. You look so at home here.

Rebecca looked up.

I mean, at peace, like you seem exactly where you should be. I don't always feel like that. Approaching the counter, she looked at the sketch on the table. Something you're working on?

One day, perhaps. Rebecca looked over at the tall sculpture of the mother and daughter. That takes all my time.

I can imagine it does. It's quite the piece of work. Elizabeth looked toward the front doors. Just how big is this place?

Two hundred and fifty acres. It used to be more, but my father donated much of it to the university. North of us.

The Jelinek campus?

Yes.

Elizabeth looked again at the large sculpture and walked to it. The impact of this is incredible. It really is. It's beautiful. How long has it taken you?

Ten months tomorrow.

Ten months?

Yes. I tend to get lost working on it, and I like that. It keeps me sane.

Sane?

You know what I mean. Would you like to see the grounds. Take a walk, perhaps?

Yes, I'd enjoy that.

Let me top our glasses up.

They walked the well-kept grounds of Jelinek Manor. Brick pathways winding through the manicured grounds lit by hundred-year-old street lamps.

It's overwhelming. It really is.

Cork.

Cork?

That made it possible. My great-grandfather. Of course, my grandfather and father were excellent stewards of what they inherited. Unlike me. I was born in that house, and I live there still.

Why unlike you?

The family stops with me. I had an older brother—he died, unmarried, no kids. She looked at Elizabeth. He was gay. He was also the most beautiful and loving person you could ever hope to meet. The good ones always seem to go too early, don't they?

Yes. It does seem like that, unfortunately.

Yes, it does. It was to be his, and his kids after that, and so forth in perpetuity. The entitlement of the Jelineks.

I'm sorry.

Thank you. And I don't either.

Don't?

Kids.

There's still time.

No, I'm afraid not. She looked back at Elizabeth. Would you like to see the main house?

Yes, I'd like that. What will you do?

Do?

With all of this?

The university. An arts and agricultural college. Coexisting.

What a wonderful idea.

I hope so. My two passions, art and animals.

They walked on, sipping their wine, Rebecca stopping and refilling their glasses, placing the empty bottle on the walkway.

Are they all yours?

Rebecca looked at the sculptures spread throughout the grounds. I wish. Some, but not all. She pointed, that's David Smith.

They came to the back door of the house, and against the wall was a small rusted silver bucket filled with broken sidewalk chalk.

Rebecca unlocked the door. I haven't been in here for such a long while myself. She looked at Elizabeth. Who knows what we'll find? Come in.

Rebecca turned the back hallway light on, the light of a large chandelier reflecting on the black and white marble tile.

While we're back here, I'll get us another bottle from the cellar. Feel free to turn the lights on and have a look around. I'll find you.

Elizabeth walked from room-to-room, turning on lights, exploring, marveling at the expanse of each room, the design and overwhelming detail. The sheer unbelievable elegance of it all.

Here we go.

Elizabeth turned and watched Rebecca walking toward her with a new bottle of wine. It's like another world. It's absolutely stunning. It really is. I'm in complete awe.

Rebecca looked around the Great Room. I suppose it is, in many ways. Or was. Although, when I was little, it was just my grandparents' house, and I loved being here.

Elizabeth looked at the different shapes of darkened shades on the wall.

Rebecca looked too. Most of it has been donated, although, I kept a few of my favorite pieces. Let me get this opened. I'll meet you in the main entrance. I'll be right there.

Elizabeth found herself in the music room, a large square room with a high ceiling, large windows overlooking a section of woods with a path running through them. She walked to the Steinway Model B grand piano with an art deco mahogany metronome. She ran her hand over the piano, walking around it, while looking out the window.

She found the main entrance and flipped the light on and walked under a large chandelier high above her, highlighting the large curved wrought iron staircase.

This is my favorite spot in the house.

Elizabeth turned and looked at Rebecca. Really? Why?

The parties. Rebecca poured them each another drink and she sat on the stairs, Elizabeth joining her.

Don't get me wrong, I fully understand and appreciate the opulence and entitlement of it all—the divide it casts. But as a young girl, I didn't understand any of that, not yet, and I loved to watch all the people coming and going. The women in their dresses, the elegance of all of that. The hellos and goodbyes. You remember those things, and they seem to stay with you. At least, they have with me.

It must have been very special.

It was. The guilt came later. I've spent my entire adulthood trying to rip it all apart, mostly in my art. That which I hold so dear in my heart. Strange, isn't it?

It must be difficult.

I don't know if difficult is the right word. Not with everything I've had. It's tragic, in many ways, I suppose. She cleared a tear from her eye.

Rebecca?

I'm fine. It can be a little overwhelming. It's been a long time.

Would you like to go?

No, I'm fine, thank you.

Why did you invite me here?

Rebecca looked at Elizabeth, and as she searched for the right words, she thought, how best to articulate reasons she couldn't fully understand herself? She took a sip of wine. I don't know. Getting dressed and going out for a morning coffee, which happens—what? Once, maybe twice a week, is the only time I do go out. And even then, it's just to ride the bike, mostly.

You've been depressed?

To say the least.

Would you like to talk about it?

No, thank you, that's not why I asked you here. She finished her glass of wine and reached for the bottle and topped up Elizabeth's glass and refilled hers. I wanted to share it with someone. She looked at Elizabeth. And I'm hoping it's all right that it's with you?

I'm flattered. It's all so very beautiful. All of it.

Yes it is. And letting go of it . . . it's the right thing to do. Let others be its keeper. Be responsible for it, without emotional investment, and the entire spectrum of that, and everything that comes with it. There's no longer anything I need or want from it. Not now. Not anymore. And honestly, it should be shared and put to better use. She cleared another tear away and looked at Elizabeth. Perhaps we should go. We'll turn the lights out and make our way back while we can still walk.

They exited the house, Rebecca locking the door.

They walked back in silence, sipping their wine. Rebecca stopped, reaching her hand out to Elizabeth's arm. Thank you.

Honestly, it was a pleasure. Thank you for asking me.

Rebecca looked at her phone. She sent a text.

Everything all right?

Yes. I'm afraid I'm going to have to work, if that's okay? Adam will take you home.

Adam?

A friend. I'm sorry I have to work, but it can't wait. Although, I feel I've made a new friend, and thank you for that.

I've had a wonderful time.

I'm glad. So have I.

They reached the studio and walked inside.

I'll get your coat.

Elizabeth finished her glass of wine and handed the glass to Rebecca and took her coat and put it on.

The sound of a motorcycle approaching.

He'll get you home safely. I couldn't possibly drive.

Thank you again.

You're welcome. Elizabeth held her arms out, and they hugged. And thank you for being so understanding about my having to cut this short. They looked at one another, Rebecca's hands lingering on Elizabeth's shoulders. It's important. I only have so much time, and I must get this done.

Elizabeth looked at the statue, and she thought for a moment. She looked back at Rebecca. You couldn't go inside alone?

Rebecca tilted her head slightly, dropping her hands from Elisabeth's shoulders.

Elizabeth nodded toward the main house.

Oh, I don't know. I wasn't planning on that, actually. It just happened. But I'm glad it did.

The bike had pulled up, Adam appearing at the door.

Thank you for coming, Adam. And thank you, again, Elizabeth. Now we can be more comfortable with one another when we see each other at the coffee place. And hopefully, you'll come back, and I won't be so rude next time.

I've enjoyed myself. I'd love to come back. Thank you, again.

Rebecca climbed the portable stairs. She stopped and looked back at Elizabeth and Adam walking out the door. She climbed the rest of the stairs, put on her welding mask, started the torch, and began to work.

Elizabeth continued to frequent the coffee shop each morning, varying her times, sometimes lingering by the counter, sometimes sitting and drinking her tea, and reading the paper.

Several months later, Elizabeth sat alone at the table by the window, starring out at all the people, thinking one of them, one day, might be Rebecca. She looked down at the paper on the table and flipped it over. There was a picture of Rebecca. The headline read: "Jelinek heiress found dead." She whispered, oh my God, no. She read the article. "On the one year anniversary of the death of her eleven-year-old daughter, Sunday Jelinek, Rebecca Jelinek, local artist and sole surviving member of the Jelinek dynasty, was found dead in her studio. Details are currently being withheld. The death, however, appears to be a suicide. Her latest sculpture, *Mother and Daughter*, is still scheduled to be unveiled at the town square during the bi-centennial celebrations, one week from tomorrow."

THERE'S A GIF THAT
PLAYS IN MY MIND

It was a sunny day and he was driving on a four-lane highway. He came upon a pickup truck pulled off to the side of the road, a transport truck parked just beyond it.

He slowed and gave the shoulder a wide berth.

There was a man on his back and he'd been cut in half. He was a large man, you could tell. There wasn't a big pool of blood, or guts, or even his legs, just his top half. The only blood he could see was in the man, mixed with the white parts of his insides. There was another man, the trucker possibly, kneeling over the one cut in half. They were talking. What the hell could they be talking about? He didn't know. He couldn't hear them.

He kept driving, the sun bright on the road before him, and he couldn't stop thinking about it. Perhaps the one cut in half had been setting the jack under his pickup when the truck driver, at that very moment of his passing, dropped something. His lighter perhaps? Or maybe he was changing the station on the radio? It could have been anything, really, when you think about it.

The rest of the way home it replayed in his mind, like a GIF, looping over and over.

On the television that night he watched a man score a touchdown. The man was happy. He tucked the football under his arm and pointed to the sky.

He clicked the TV off and went to bed and both images began to play in his mind. The man kneeling over the one cut in half, talking—what'd they say? The ballplayer, happy, pointing to the sky.

He woke early and headed out in his boat. He pulled into a little bay, the fog heavy, the morning still dark. He threw a cast and leaned back, crossing his feet over the gunnel. He sipped his coffee and the images came, the man kneeling over the one cut in half, talking—what'd they say? The ballplayer, happy, pointing to the sky.

A fish hit and he set the hook, the line running out, the fish jumping and arcing in the early morning fog. The images played. The man kneeling over the one cut in half, talking—what'd they say? The ballplayer, happy, pointing to the sky. He looked at the fish still arced above the water, frozen in time, somehow, and a new image came, of himself, cooking the fish in a frying pan beneath a clear blue sky, turning and looking back at himself. The fish suddenly threw the hook and the line fell limp, the boat drifting in the quiet foggy bay, the images playing, the man kneeling over the one cut in half, talking—what'd they say? The ballplayer, happy, pointing to the sky. The one of himself, cooking the fish in a frying pan beneath a clear blue sky, turning and looking back at himself. Over and over. The boat drifting. The images. The boat drifting—gone, in the early morning fog of the quiet bay.

IN THE LONG NIGHTS OF OUR NEVER ENOUGH

You are beautiful and you are there and you reside in me yet.

I see the tub you take. It's warm and it's scented, and it's meant to help with your uncertainties. Calm your anxiety and anticipation. And it does. Not completely, of course, but somewhat. You sip your wine and close your eyes and lean back, your long black hair falling over the back of the tub, and I watch you cry.

You step from the tub and towel yourself dry.

You put on your heavy white bathrobe and start down the dark narrow hallway. Slow uncertain steps. Little ones. You reach out and touch the wall and steady yourself.

I watch you sit at the end of our bed and rest. Your resolve is slipping, and you remind yourself, this is something you can do. That you need to do.

You brush your hair, long slow strokes. These days that are not those days and never will be again.

You look to the window. The day's light has begun to fade. You stand and walk to the dresser and pick up the pile of things you placed there earlier. You carry them to the bed and your robe falls open. You look in the mirror. Still young—just, and only just, and you need this.

In your hands is a black lace and silk G-string. You slip your legs through the thin straps. You put on a black garter and sit on the bed and roll up one black stocking and then the other one. You stand and put on your bra, my desire holding you—and you lean into this wanting. Your eyes closed, remembering. As I do too.

You look amazing, but there is no one there to tell you, and so I whisper it to you.

You walk back to the dresser and finish the glass of red wine you started in the tub. You place the empty glass on the dresser and put on your jewelry, all fake, but nevertheless, it shines and glitters, and it will do.

You apply your red lipstick.

Your perfume.

You're downstairs, and it's past time. You should have left already. You look in the long hallway mirror at your short tight black dress that still fits well. Your high black leather boots. Your long coat. You look in the mirror again, and before you change your mind you open the door to the cold dark discontent of this winter night, and it takes you.

A wind picks up and you look at the moving trees in the night. At the winter moon. You put your hand to your hair to stop it from blowing. You walk faster and hope no one can see you. But why should you care? But you do—of course you do, and you just wish you could fuck off for a change from being you.

You'd like to disappear, covered in the cold darkness of this night. And you mustn't start to cry. You look again at the moving trees, at the branches without leaves. Dead and gone and please— why? Why'd you do it? Take such risks?

Love and hope and never enough.

You didn't know. How could I tell you? My flaws together with our brilliance in that moving above you. These desires of our wanting.

Come to me. One last time. Please.

A car is parked in front of a coffee shop, blue smoke choking in the cold beneath a street light.

There's a driver by the door.

You approach and he opens the back door. The sound of the door closing makes you jump.

The car pulls out and you watch the town moving before you. A world that was once ours. Loving and living without thought. And why was that not enough?

There's a fully stocked bar, help yourself.

You thank him in a voice you know he cannot hear and you pour a glass of red wine. You look out the window—to this world now. Which is what? Alone and broke and the kids gone. Don't shake and don't start to cry, and you take another sip. The wine is warm and it's soothing, and it helps settle your nerves. But only just enough. You look at your arm and the faded scars there and you finish your wine and lean your head back and close your eyes: all of us happy, and together again.

You hate being exposed like this. Being seen. Don't you? Dead inside and being seen.

I didn't handle it so well. I don't think I knew how, or if I even wanted to.

You look back out the window. The kids are with your parents. Did you know that?

Crowds of people. So many people. All with purpose, or so it seems.

You'd hate that, wouldn't you? What was I to do? I wasn't stable enough, that's what they said. How could I be? I wasn't even that when you were here, was I?

And now you think, don't make this car stop, please. Keep driving.

The two of us, in this car. In this forever night.

The car pulls up to a hotel washed in bright lights. The driver opens the door and you see her. She is stunning. More beautiful than you remember. Her dress and blonde hair. Her jewelry—all of her, dripping and glittering beneath a long open faux fur coat.

She takes you by the arm. Your heart is racing. You feel light headed. She looks at you. Don't worry, you'll do fine, and she walks you inside.

The suite is large and dimly lit. You walk through the room and through a set of open double doors and this room is darker yet with just one soft light spilling out from a single lamp next to a large poster bed.

You watch her walk to an empty chair and remove her coat and place it there. She looks at you and you go to her. She takes your coat and places it with hers.

She turns you around and unzips your dress. You look back at her and she looks at you.

Your dress falls to the floor. Still in your heels, and you step out from it.

She moves you to the bed.

Put her on her hands and knees.

You look toward the voice—in the corner, in the dark shadows. You look at her and she stands waiting. You climb onto the high bed, on your hands and knees, and you can make this stop. You know you can. You close your eyes and for a moment nothing happens. No one speaks. Your heart pounding.

And now the certainty of her comes, scented. Her curves. Lace and warm skin. Next to you. Pressing to you. It feels warm. It feels good. And it doesn't feel wrong. You want that. All of it. Her pressing to you more. Cover me. And in that darkness there is what?

She's kissing you. You open your eyes and look at her, feeling yourself giving over to the light touch of her soft glossed lips calming you. Her hand coming to your leg. Moving up your leg.

She moves behind you, her hands coming to your hips and pushing you forward, your head lower, your hair falling before you. The heel of her hand pressing into your back. The nails of her other hand drawing across your skin. You close your eyes and lower your head to the pillow, and you want more. And why shouldn't you? Feel good and have this and want more.

The bed lowers.

You lift your head.

His large, cold hands come to your hips and you brace yourself. She takes your head in her hands and you look at her—your head snapping back, and you gasp.

His grip is harder, pulling you to him. You close your eyes and lower your head, his full weight coming to you, your arms stiffening, and you don't dare move. Your tears come.

The shower runs.

Bills on a table.

The car is there.

You walk together washed in the hard lights of the hotel, stopping at the open car door.

You did fine. I'll call you tomorrow. She kisses your cheek. Get some rest.

The car moves through the night and you lean back in the leather seat and close your eyes, my face fading in your mind.

You can't hold it.

No, not yet, please. You cry again, and you look out the window. To the darkness. Your reflection there, in the glass.

In these long nights of our never enough.

A LOOK BACK AND
SAY GOODBYE

He sat on a bench in the town square and opened a beer. He took a sip and wondered, in the church of our knowing, the blood runs, it always runs, in the streets of our towns and the streets of our hearts.

He shaded his eyes to the rim of the sun low in the sky before him. He saw an old man with a shopping cart, stopped, smoking down a cigarette, looking off somewhere else.

And he thought, you were to stay in your rooms, but you didn't, you came to the door.

Why?

Bye, Mom.

I told em, in the dark, in the cold, she can't hear you, your head bouncing against my back, long hair hanging down, your wrists bandaged, little emptied plastic bottles jangling in my pockets.

Beyond the intensity of the darkness, of that night, these real nights of us, there was no road to follow.

We turned around.

You slept for two days and your heart didn't stop.

We knew the storm was coming and I had only just beat it out getting into town and back to get some things we needed.

I gave you your pill and waited until you were out.

It was one of those times it didn't work.

You were sitting on the couch with the kids watching a movie, both wrists opened up, two puddles of blood on the floor.

She's been talking gibberish.

What is madness and how did it find us? A last chance to reach out and find some handles and hold on?

How long?

Fight harder.

Be stronger.

A weakness in the heart of knowing, so much of everyone's truth.

He took another sip of beer and stretched his legs out and crossed his boots and in his mind he searched for her, the very essence of her; her scent; her touch, all of her, and all that he wanted again right now, covering him—that calming.

On the porch stairs, you were there. The sun warming on your face, watching the kids walking down the long, shaded driveway. Walking and talking, playing, stopping to see the horses come to the post and rail fence to see them off. The horses' tails flicking at flies, the school bus honking and waiting.

You wore faded and ripped jeans, a white tank top, and we stretched back to the warm porch boards and made love in the sunlight.

We smoked and we talked, time passing in our words like a faint breeze across our world—a world no longer ours in the making. The fog in your brain coming, going away, coming back, and settling again.

And it couldn't be stopped.

Not by me, your doctors, meds, not by the letting of your own blood.

It would come.

He finished his beer and took another from his pocket and opened it.

Like the lily and the rose.

Je me souviens.

Like it never will be again.

He looked across the blurred square. We were always together though, weren't we, Lizzy? Even then—always then, reaching, that same sun, same big sky, sheltering us, lazy and lingering in the tall grass by the big shady river. The purity of your heart bringing to us the rhythm of everything good.

He looked at the store that sold the beer. It was closed. He took another sip and leaned forward and put his finger to the dirt and wrote the words, In the wind: A refrain.

He spat to the dirt and lit a cigarette.

That night.

You drank a bottle of red wine, you took another one with you, and you drove away. You drove down a dark country road and you drove onto an irrigated field of beans and you ran a jagged piece of green glass across your wrists.

They said you wouldn't make it. But you did. You stayed.

He shook the match out and tossed it to the ground, and he thought about that, what it must have been like, stopped, all that emptiness and darkness coming and settling upon you.

In the dark.

In the quiet.

Waiting.

He took a drag of his cigarette and kicked dirt onto the smouldering match. You wrote a note in red ink on the back of a cigarette pack, and I couldn't make it out, what it is you wrote. Not really.

He looked at the old man, stopped, looking back at him.

That was the hardest part, wasn't it, Lizzy? That knowing. The slash and burn of so many sharp declines, the going heavy in the darkness, and always waiting, the certainty of it coming, with little to do but try to make it through.

He took a drag of his cigarette and dropped it to the ground and toed it out. You woke from a late morning nap and walked to the window, watching for a while, crisp red-brown leaves whirling and tumbling down the vacant road.

You looked at me, and I could see it, the very same as if it were an object you held in your hands before me. Your wellness had surrendered, betraying you again, our hopes held tight beneath warm sheets in the night—gone. Fallen away again.

He heard the old man's cart start up with its one squeaky wheel and he watched him push it down a narrow, shaded laneway.

Blood on the sheets, on the curtains, on the floor, down the hallway.

Here now, and with us still.

An altered state that became a constant, and it shouldn't have been.

There were no other options.

Why?

It's a good question, one you can hold up to the light and never be satisfied with what the reflections of you are trying to see.

An unrelenting death repetitiveness that you and your children could not stop.

They'd wash your current meds out and start a new round, something different. Anything. But it wouldn't hold, it never did.

He watched the old man disappear, the squeak of the wheel still coming to him like some demented whistle moving over the empty courtyard, and settling before him. He leaned forward, his hand open to it, grabbing hold of it, and it made him feel better, choking the calling of it until it was rung out and gone. He opened his hand and dropped the deadness of it to the ground.

Once everything had failed, every possible combination of meds, all those rounds of ECT, everything changed, the being diagnosed as Treatment Resistant became a divide. The four to six week stays in the hospital, being moved to a university hospital specializing in mental disorders and studied for three months, it all stopped.

We so easily sacrifice science to the altar of our beliefs, and yet, we hide behind it, too, filling voids, segregating ourselves. Scapegoating. Because if we didn't, we'd be forced to examine the other side of us, the collective side, the uncomfortable truth that it is all of us together.

One in five, how could it not be?

Locked in cold dead rooms with restraints.

Looking at you through heavy glass.

Little harmless beautiful you.

"I can show you how to kill yourself, if you really want to die."

Why?

"You're taking up a bed someone who wants to live could use."

All too true and far too prevalent.

You escaped triage, broke out and ran, over Fiddler's Green, picked up in the night by the police, and it did not matter if it was the hospital you fled because you needed to be there, you were charged and arrested and set free in the morning to the world, barefoot.

He took another sip of beer and thought, I really don't care who you are, how old you are, your understandings, your beliefs, lack of them, healthcare professional, or not, family, or not—take your bootstraps and keep walking.

He looked again in the direction of the squeaky wheel sound that was not there now, the square lonelier for its absence, the stillness and silence heavier.

We'd moved to that little house in town to be closer to bigger hospitals and family. I went down into the basement, and I can't remember why. And I've tried. Over and over, I've tried. I came back up and you were gone. And it wasn't like before, there were too many places for you to go—too many side streets, dead-ends, parks, and strip malls.

They found you, Lizzy. Not me.

Not that time.

And there you were—alone again in the night, parked behind an empty building.

Why that?

Always that?

Did I do it? Put that there? Empty bottles squeezed tight at your feet.

I couldn't do it, be your witness, and I'm sorry about that, even though you wanted me to.

No one was stronger, fought harder, or longer. Not that I know of. And you deserved that witness, and I guess I was that, just not how you needed me to be.

Not in the end I wasn't.

Where's that sound, old man? Bring it back. Break the emptiness, and I'll be your witness and you be mine.

He looked at the sun, almost gone and taking everything with it.

Lizzy?

Bravery is caring. It's understanding the weakness in the heart of all our truth and still caring.

Lizzy?

And I wonder if you can understand that?

I'm right here, Finn.

I sat in the car one time, did you know that?

No. When?

I put you in the backseat, all torn up, and I didn't drive, not right away I didn't. I just sat there, wanting to yell—scream, so fucking loud.

But who was there to hear me? That's what I didn't know.

There was no one, that's who.

What about God, Finn?

He turned and looked in the direction of the old man who was not there now.

What would you have said to Him?

I don't know, Lizzy. I guess I would've said, hold on, what's going on?

And what would He have said to you?

He looked at the coming darkness and thought, healthcare for humanity, how hard can that be to understand? Love and caring, Lizzy, that's what He'd have said.

Yes, Finn, love and caring. It's all we have and all that's required.

No, Lizzy, all we have is the cold hard reach of science, new meds, and go home.

The old man was there, standing next to him, and he thought, how'd you get there? And he watched the old man tip his head back and close his eyes, scenting the coming winds, much the same as a dog might do.

He looked at the low, dark clouds moving quickly above him, the old man disappearing again across the darkening square, the sound of the squeaky wheel drifting and fading with the falling sun.

Will it never stop?

Say goodbye.

No, not today.

Say goodbye. It's all that's left.

He heard a cricket and he looked to a patch of dead weeds coming up from the dirt. He leaned his head back and closed his eyes and let the coming darkness take him. And it did, and in his mind, he ran, once again, these dark and empty streets of our hearts.

He felt a warm breeze, a light touch, a whispering: In the guardianship of perfect silence all shall be known.

He opened his eyes, unable to distinguish himself from the darkness, and you were there, with him now, your eyes so clear and blue, your long black hair, red lips.

The old man, farther down in the square, stopped, looking back at their feet entwined, moving over the empty courtyard.

Under the moonlight.

Dancing.

As if touched as one by the stain of this life.

All their moments spent.

The man:

In the dark.

In the quiet.

Waiting.

IN DEATH I DREAM OF YOU YET
(A LOOK BACK AND SAY GOODBYE, ALTERNATIVE VERSION)

See me dying, withered and decaying between crisp white sheets. I wait for the prick of the needle—it comes, the warm reprieve taking me again.

And I run, these dark and empty city streets.

Stopping, my heart pounding and resounding in my head, I watch thin pools of water gathered upon the road beginning to ripple. I look behind me, an immeasurable distance back to the birthplace of darkness itself. I turn back and a two-headed dog with massive jaws that foam and drip sinks both sets of jaws deep into my face. We fall to the cobblestone surface, the skank dampness of its fur—the trapped stale winds of all our yesterdays, upon me. My faceless head lulls forward and the dog takes it. The heads, growling and snapping, fight to enter my red, dark hole, and they hollow me out.

They rip and consume the skin from my bones and they eat the bones so that all remains of me is a skull dripping in blood from a scalp that is nothing more than a few splotches of dark hair.

And now I see you, sitting at the end of our bed, wrapped in your heavy white bathrobe, your skin fresh and pink from a warm tub. And even with the stain of this life worn so heavy upon you,

you are beautiful. Your blue eyes, long black hair, lips that crave red lipstick, still all shine, despite the fog that settles at the front of your brain, goes away, comes back, and settles again.

I open my eyes—where? The room silent and heavy with the smell of my pending death.

And I remember. Together on the porch stairs, leaning back, the sun warming on our faces, watching our four young children walking down our long, shaded driveway. Walking and talking, playing, stopping to see the horses come to the post and rail fence to see them off. The horses' tails flicking at flies, the school bus honking and waiting.

We smoked and we talked, time passing in our words like a faint breeze across our world—a world that was once ours in the making.

You wore faded and ripped jeans and a white tank top and we laid back on the warm porch boards and made love in the sunlight.

That night, you drank a bottle of red wine. You took another one with you, and you drove away. You drove down a dark country road. You drove onto an irrigated field of beans and you ran a jagged piece of green glass across your wrists.

They said you wouldn't make it. That's what they said. But you did. You stayed.

And now the children are here, I know they are, I can feel them, standing before me, so beautiful, still and quiet, their sad young eyes filled with such fear and uncertainty.

And I want to tell them, all the world is yours.

I open my eyes and try to speak but the needle comes, and I go, once again.

You woke from a late morning nap and walked to the chair by the small side window and sat looking out at a cool autumn day without sun. You watched for a while, crisp red-brown leaves, whirling and tumbling down the vacant road. You looked at me, and I could see it, the very same as if it were an object you held in your hands before me. Your wellness surrendering. Betraying you again. Our hopes held tight beneath warm sheets in the night—gone. Fallen away again.

And this pain, it wouldn't be put off, not by me, your doctors, meds, not by the letting of your own blood.

It would come, and it never would not come.

You drew a warm tub and drank a glass of red wine, and you leaned your head back, crying, long and silent, once again.

You put on your heavy white bathrobe and walked to our room and sat at the end of our bed.

I dream I wake and see you there, and you are beautiful.

We talk and we laugh, twenty years warmed by the sun breaking through the open window, and we stay like this, for a very long time.

Somewhere in the house the kids yell and scream. One of us should go. Please, I hear myself saying, stay. The tears that come now are mine.

I think back to that day not long after we moved to this little house in town. I wasn't yet sick. I went down into the basement. I can't remember why. And I've tried, over and over, I've tried. I came back up and you were gone. And it wasn't like at the farm, there were too many places for you to go—too many side streets, dead ends, parks, and strip malls.

They found you in the night, parked behind a building. Empty bottles squeezed tight at your feet.

Did I do that? Put those there?

I open my eyes, unable to distinguish myself from the darkness.

A warm touch upon my face.

A whisper: In the guardianship of perfect silence, all shall be known.

And now your eyes come, so clear and blue, and there's a breeze, your long hair swaying, your red lips before me, our feet entwined, twisting and twirling in soft white sand on a vast empty beach I have never seen before. And we dance, as if touched as one by the stain of this life. A dance of time. All our moments spent.

SPECIAL THANKS

With love and ongoing appreciation ...

John and Nancy, Kim and Liz, Dave and Julie,

Megan,

Grant, Tim, Charlie and Delores, Kimberly, Adam,

Melissa,

Kaaren.

PUBLISHING ACKNOWLEDGMENTS

(In order as they appear here.)

"Under a Big Moon" .*Cent Magazine,* 05/12/18.

"Blood-Red on the Bay" *Wilderness House Literary Review,* 11/25/17. *Chaleur Magazine, 03/01/19.*

"An Old Man and a Boy: Samuel's Story" *Wilderness House Literary Review,* 02/18/18.

"You Are a Child of God Too" *Wilderness House Literary Review,* 12/12/16.

"In A Small Town (Called America)" *XRAY Literary Magazine,* 12/01/19.

"Under the Midnight Sun" *Kingston University of London: Words, Pauses, Noises,* 04/24/16. *Toyon: Multilingual Journal of Literature and Art Humboldt State University* 03/20. Eric Hoffer Award, Best New Writing, finalist, 2015.

"On the Prairie, West of the Third Meridian" *Litro Magazine, US Edition,* 04/28/19.

"Liars on the Run" *Anti-Heroin Chic,* 08/01/20.

"Riding a Bike through the Lonely Continuum of Time" *XRAY Literary Magazine*, 09/18/20

"cash, guns, booze and whores: Desperation Never Wins" *The Prague Review, 02/14/16.*

"The Lighthouse, the Pier and the Woman" *Spark, A Creative Anthology*, 06/11/13. *Kind Writers Anthology*, 08/01/20.

"On My Way to Sunday" *University Collage of Dublin, HCE Review,* 04/10/19.

"There's a GIF That Plays in My Mind" *Carnival Magazine*, 11/01/13.

"In The Long Nights of Our Never Enough" *Mugwump Press Anthology: Hotel*, 02/03/17.

"In Death I Dream of You Yet" *Indigo Rising UK, 07/01/13. Liquid Imagination, 12/01/14. Stigma Fighters, 08/08/15.*

Made in the USA
Middletown, DE
17 July 2022

69179908R00094